Light Riders and the Missouri Mud Murder

Books by Ann I. Goldfarb

The Face Out of Time

Ripple Rider: An Anguillan Adventure in Time

The Last Tag

———❧———

The Light Rider Series:

Light Riders and the Morenci Mine Murder

Light Riders and the Fleur-de-lis Murder

**TWO
CATS
PRESS**

Light Riders and the Missouri Mud Murder

A Time Travel Mystery by
Ann I. Goldfarb

*For my brother, Dr. Stephen S. Scher, whose
June 21, 1962 gift of **Historical Geology**
opened the vast mysteries of geological time for
me and set my imagination on fire for decades
to come.*

Introduction

University of Missouri, Department of Geological Sciences Office of Professor Howard Langston, Paleontological, Sedimentological and Stratigraphy Studies, Present Day

Professor Howard Langston stared at the email on his computer screen and shook his head.

"This can't be right. There's got to be a major malfunction with the mass spectrometer in the Radiometric Lab."

Then, leaning back in his chair, he shouted across the room to his assistant.

"Cal, do me a favor and give the Radiometric Lab a call. I think they've got a problem."

"Sure, boss. What's up?"

"Remember that fossil we uncovered a few months ago near Springfield? The partial saber-tooth skull with the small round hole near the eye socket?"

"Yeah, how could I forget? If I didn't know any better, I would have sworn that it was made by a bullet."

"Apparently, you're not the only one. The lab results I just got back indicated that there were fragments of lead alloy in the skull."

"Lead alloy? You've got to be kidding me. That skull is over a million years old. That's impossible."

"Not according to the lab. They even sent the sample for neutron activation analysis. That's how they were able to determine the type and age of the metal."

"Then something's wrong with their equipment."

"That's what I'm saying. I mean, let's face it. The saber-tooth tiger lived in the Ice Age and the last I knew, humans with guns weren't hunting them. I'm going to ask the lab to send the sample to another university for testing."

"Where do you suggest?"

"All of these labs are top-notch. University of Wisconsin, Ohio State, Elemental Analysis at Texas A & M..."

"I've got a friend at Texas A & M. Let me make the call. I'm sure it's just a malfunction with something in our lab."

"Must be. Because the only other plausible explanation isn't plausible at all."

"You mean..."

"I mean, let's leave that one for the guys in quantum physics."

Prologue:
Ryn

M y head felt as if someone had just clobbered it with a broom, and trying to stand upright became an Olympic feat. The dense brush that surrounded me made it difficult to figure out exactly where we were. Then I heard Aeden's voice.

"When we get out of this weird swampy-woodsy area, we've got to find clothing for the right time period. It's the late 1940s or early 50s right? My clothes are all wrong. All wrong."

I pushed some of the thicker leaves away from my face and took a step forward. I wasn't exactly sure of the place, but I knew the era.

"Clothing? You're worried about your clothes fitting in?" I screamed, unable to control the pitch in my voice. "Take a look around Aeden, but do not move. I mean it. DO NOT MOVE. And clothing should be the last thing on your mind."

I could hear my sister gasp as she saw the same thing I did—a ten-foot tall mastodon quietly chewing leaves off of a tree that stood only a few feet from us. And that wasn't the worst thing. Someone else had slipped back in time with us.

PART ONE:
SOLAR FLARES

Chapter One:
Aeden

❧

My mother had the cell phone glued to her ear and even if Ryn were to scream at the top of his lungs, I doubt she would have paid attention.

"Encased in mud? How dreadful. Awful, really. I'm so sorry, Evie. How's your family taking the news? …Uh huh, uh huh….Oh, that's just horrid…No, I really do understand…. What? You'll have to speak louder. It's those darn solar flares. They're interfering with everything. So what did the coroner say? Oh, uh huh…Evie, I feel so bad for you. After all those years. Imagine. And now to find out he was murdered. The whole town thought he had—. Never mind. And… "

Ryn kept approaching her, only to be motioned away by her hand.

"What's going on? Mom's been on that phone for hours and I really need to borrow the car. I told Linna that I was going to pick her up in 15 minutes and that was a half an hour ago!"

"Try waving your driver's license in front of her. You've had plenty of practice shoving it under my nose every chance you get."

"Whoa—what put you in such a bad mood?"

"I'm not in a bad mood, I just have tons of homework and I still haven't learned all my lines for 'Stage Door.' The performance is in less than a month."

"Is that why you keep walking around muttering about the stupid calla lilies being in bloom? I swear, Aeden, I know all the lines and I'm not in the play! Why doesn't the theater department ever produce something exciting?"

"You wouldn't understand, Ryn. All you know how to do is throw a ball, catch a ball and run after a ball. A dog could do that!"

"But a dog wouldn't have one of these, would he? Want me to show you my license again?"

"Leave me alone Ryn and go bother Mom for the car."

"She just keeps shushing me and shooing me away. Honestly, what can be so important?"

"I don't know Ryn, but whatever it is, it doesn't sound good. She's talking to Evie Montgomery. You know, our old neighbor. We haven't seen her in years. Not since they moved back to some little town in Missouri."

"Yeah. I always liked Logan. He must be in college by now. And Ajay? I wonder if she's just as spoiled as she was back in elementary school?"

"Probably. And I don't think you'll have to wonder for long. From the way Mom's talking, I think she'll want us to go there."

"WHAT? WHY?"

"You really have to ask? Put the words together. Coroner. Murder. Mud. Some guy died and somehow we're going to get involved. Just when I get a lead role in a school play. I've waited how many years for this? I only hope I'm wrong."

"Crap. She's still talking. You'd better be wrong about this, Aeden, because I don't want to be dragged off to who-knows-where Missouri either. We're in the middle of lacrosse season. I'm not going anywhere!"

Just then, my mother gave us a weird look and walked over to the corner desk in the kitchen where she throws her bag. Next thing I knew, she reached into it, handed Ryn the keys and mouthed, "Be back by 7:00 for dinner." She didn't even bother to ask where he was going. She just kept talking on the phone with Evie Montgomery.

I figured Ryn and Linna were going to watch the tail end of the girls' softball game or just hang out somewhere. It was a school night and even if my mother was pre-occupied with whatever murder took place in Missouri, Ryn wasn't about to blow his chances using the car. He'd be back in time for dinner.

I got up from the table, grabbed the script and walked past the kitchen to the living room.

"The calla lilies are in bloom again. Such a strange flower. Suitable to any occasion. I carried them on my wedding day and now I place them here in memory of something that has died."

It turned out I was right after all and Ryn wasn't taking it too well. He argued during dinner, after dinner and even when he stormed upstairs to go to bed. I made a few feeble attempts at it, too, complaining that I'd miss play practice. But nothing we said seemed to matter. We were going to Missouri all right, even if it was just for a long weekend.

I was about to turn off the light by my bed when Ryn knocked on the door and walked in before I could even say anything.

"Can you believe this? We're flying all the way to Missouri for a weekend just because someone's relative died. It's bad enough we have to traipse all over the world when our own dead relatives appear out of nowhere, but this...this is someone else's dead relative! And they've been dead for years! It's not like it just happened!"

"Well, in a way, it did. I mean, they found the guy all mummified in mud and the coroner thinks he may have been murdered. And it's not just any relative, it's Evie Montgomery's grandfather. And you know how close she and Mom are. They're practically sisters. Besides, it's just for a long weekend. We have Monday off anyway for a teachers' conference day."

"I know. I planned on spending the day with Linna, not the mummified remains of Evie Montgomery's grandfather. And you know what's worse? We'll have to spend the weekend with Ajay."

I could feel my stomach slowly churning. The last time I saw Ajay Montgomery was six years ago. We were in the same fifth grade class and I could barely stand her then.

"Maybe she's changed. People do change, you know."

Ryn made a face.

"Yeah, she's probably gone from being a princess to being queen-empress or something. I'll tell you one thing, I'm not spending any time with her."

"We may have to. Mom will be all caught up in the murder thing and we'll get stuck having to keep Ajay company. And Dad won't even be there. He's stuck in Minneapolis for a conference."

"This really stinks, Aeden, especially the Ajay part."

I should have just agreed and said good-night, but I opened my mouth and once the words came out, I couldn't stop them.

"We don't *have* to stay with Ajay. We know how to find out who killed her great-grandfather. We could make it work this time."

"After Paris I thought you never wanted to do that again."

"Ryn, I'd rather be at the Salem Witch Trials than spend a weekend with Ajay!"

"I'm holding you to that, Aeden. Sleep tight."

Then he closed the door and I immediately regretted everything I had said, but it was too late.

Chapter Two:
Ryn

Ajay's voice was even more irritating than I remembered. Like fingernails ripping their way down a chalkboard. And, as if that wasn't enough, she was so loud that her voice penetrated the entire baggage claim area.

"Ryn! Aeden! How was your flight? I haven't seen you in ages! You guys look great!"

"We're fine, Ajay," I muttered. "It's uh, nice to see you, too."

Aeden gave her one of those false hugs that are reserved for great aunts and elderly grandparents. I pointed to the carousel and started to turn away.

"Looks like our bags are circling around. I'm going to grab them. I think Mom and Evie are already waiting by the exit. You two probably have a lot of catching up to do."

Aeden gave me a nasty look and turned back to Ajay, who was still talking.

"I really, really wanted you and Ryn to stay with us. Ryn could have used Logan's room. Logan won't be back from college for weeks. And you and I could have shared my room."

I left it to Aeden to explain that we would be staying near-by at a local "Inn and Suites" and that we'd be picking up a rental car in the morning. I figured Ajay would have stopped talking by the time we got into Evie's car, but I was wrong.

"Can you imagine? My great-grandfather murdered and mummified? The whole thing just gives me the creeps. What if the murderer is still alive? What if they're not done? You know, we really should have an alarm system for our house or at least a guard dog."

Evie let out one of those long sighs as if she had heard this conversation before.

"It happened years ago, Ajay. Long before you were born. In fact, your great-grandfather disappeared in 1952, right after Grandma was born. His murder couldn't possibly have anything to do with us today. It's a cold case. But one that the police want to investigate. And honestly, I don't know what I could possibly tell them. I'm just so sorry that my mother died last year. She always believed that they'd learn the truth. If she only knew…"

I sat there, waiting for it. Waiting for Ajay or her mother to get so emotional that they'd both break down and start crying. Geez. I was trapped. Trapped in the back seat with Ajay and a 45-minute drive to their home. Aeden was no help. I looked over and could see that she was getting that stupid teary-eyed look in her face. The same look she gets when that commercial about the homeless dogs comes on. It was awful. I took a short breath and spoke.

"So...how exactly was he murdered? A bullet? A knife? Poison?"

"Ryn!" my mother exclaimed. "How can you be so callous?"

But before I could say anything, Evie answered my question.

"It's OK. It's not a secret. The coroner found a bullet lodged in the back of my grandfather's head. A bullet from a .38 revolver."

I let the air escape from my chest and continued.

"Well, at least they know the murder weapon. A good CSI team could probably put the clues together in no time."

"Ryn, this isn't TV," my mother said. "It's a small town in the middle of Missouri and they don't have the resources that big cities do."

I wasn't about to argue about resources, forensic teams or murder weapons for that matter. There was only one thought in my mind—motive. Someone needed a good motive to kill Ajay's great-grandfather. And the only way the police would figure it out was to stumble on it. All I needed to do was give them a good push. Otherwise, the case would get dragged out, talked out and worn out long before it was solved. And that meant we might have to return to Missouri. Then I remembered what Aeden had said a few nights ago. *We know how to find out who killed her great-grandfather.*

So, rather than facing a weekend of Ajay bawling and my mother and Evie getting all worked up, I decided to take my sister up on her offer. At least this time we had a year—1952. A short trip back if nothing got in our way.

It was after midnight at the "Inn and Suites" when I heard Aeden knocking at my door. Good thing I was still up.

"You've got to do something, Ryn. I don't think I can stand an entire weekend with Ajay and it's only Friday night! For heaven's sake, she showed me all of the designer clothes in her closet while you and her dad went out to get the pizzas. Designer clothes! And if that wasn't bad enough, she had to shove her new iPad in my face and tell me how outdated my stuff was."

"No kidding."

"So what do we do? Tomorrow she's supposed to show us around the town while Mom and Evie meet with the police."

"A whole day to walk down one block?"

"If they have a clothing store, that'll take at least three hours!"

"OK, here's the deal. All we need is sunlight, a mirror and access to a heavy-duty prism or a series of smaller ones. We lucked out last year in Paris with the Louvre Pyramid. But I'm not so sure in this godforsaken place."

"Didn't you pack any of Auntie Zanne's prisms?"

"You saw my bag. I packed underwear and two shirts. Oh yeah, and my toothbrush. Besides, to do it Auntie Zanne's way, we'd need access to a large field or yard, and if we could do that, then we wouldn't need to get away from Ajay in the first place."

"Still, don't you want to go back and find the killer? We were so close the last time."

"So close? It was almost a 300 year difference. Close? The only thing we were close to was a guillotine! But yeah, I think we can do it this time. That main street must have at least one or two girlie shops, the kind that smell of cinnamon and candles. Those places sell glass figurines. If you take out your mirror, we could do this."

"And the timing? We won't be 300 years apart?"

"It's a matter of light and angles. Think of it like a pool table. In order to hit the balls and make sure they wind up in the right pocket, you've got to figure out the angle. Time travel is no different. The only reason we got messed up last time is because that stupid kid bumped into us and changed the angle. We'll be more careful this time. By the way, did Ajay ever tell you what her great-grandfather did for a living or anything about him for that matter?"

"All I know is that he worked for the Missouri Department of Transportation. Ajay said that he was a big shot with the 'Highway Modernization and Expansion Program.'"

"Well, maybe someone didn't want the state modernized or expanded."

"So they shot him?"

"Could be. Or...maybe it was something more personal...Anyway, let's hope Ajay gets pre-occupied with clothing or whatever else she wants to buy so we can find out for ourselves."

"You're sure it will work this time?"

"Yeah, I'm sure."

But I'm also a pretty good liar. I didn't need Aeden getting all freaked out. It was bad enough that my mom, her friend Evie, and Ajay were all becoming basket cases over a murder that took place decades ago. I knew one thing. Even if we wound up in a different time period, the time-space continuum would bring us back. It always has before. What could possibly mess it up now?

Chapter Three:
Aeden

Ajay stopped under a sign that read "Wildflower Nail Salon" and gave me a strange look.

"I'll only be a few minutes, Aeden. Maybe a half hour at the most. But I've got to get my nails touched up. Just look at them! The dark mauve polish on the tips has started to chip. You and Ryn should go into the stores. There's 'Honey and Holly,' 'The Little Cinnabun Pastry,' and we even have a book store—'The Bookery Nookery.'"

Ryn was already down the block, eyeballing the windows, but I knew he wasn't interested in tea assortments, spices or books for that matter. Evie and my mom were going to pick us up once they were done at the police station. Then, we were all going to go bowling. I couldn't imagine a worse afternoon.

"We'll be fine, Ajay. Go get your nails done. Look for us in the bookstore, OK?"

Ajay nodded and walked across the street to a small nail salon that was wedged between an insurance company and a health food store. I didn't waste any time catching up to Ryn.

"We've got a reprieve. She'll be tied up for at least 30 minutes. Any luck finding a store with crystal figurines?"

"Not yet, but 'The Sun Catcher' looks promising," Ryn said as he pointed to a fairly large storefront a few feet away. The colorful decorations in the windows and the balloons that bounced in front of the door made me think of a carnival. Whoever owned the store certainly wanted to lure in the customers. I opened the door and started to walk inside when Ryn grabbed my arm.

"Just give me a second or two. I've been trying to text Linna all morning but I keep losing the connection. Lost call. Lost service. What kind of hell hole are we in? I'm going to try her again."

"Mom was saying something the other day about the phone service and solar flares. Maybe the flares are wreaking havoc on cell phone communications."

"Well, they're not exactly helping my relationship with Linna. She's already pissed that I had to leave for the weekend when we had plans."

"Just hurry up. I'll start to look around."

I don't usually hold my breath when I walk into a store, but in this case I had no choice. The aisles were tight and the shelves were filled with china collectibles, small delicate crystal figurines, plates, mugs, trivets, and anything that could be broken with just one small bump. I walked around cautiously. Glancing out the front window I could see that Ryn was still outside. From the look on his face I knew he hadn't connected with Linna.

"Be careful," I said as he pushed open the door, "everything's breakable."

Just then, I heard a voice from the back of the store.

"Welcome to 'The Sun Catcher'. I'll be with you in a few minutes. I'm helping another customer."

"We're fine," I yelled back. Then, I moved quickly to Ryn and took my small mirror out of my purse.

"We've got to hurry before the clerk gets here."

The sunlight was beginning to reflect off of the tiny figurines of clowns, dogs and birds and the angles seemed to stretch out across the store. Ryn took the mirror from me and centered it on one of the beams, making sure that we were right next to each other. I quickly stashed my purse under one of the shelves and took a deep breath. *We've done this before. It'll be OK.*

At first I could see a faint flickering of light, and then the colors seemed to cascade all around us in waves. Slow, undulating waves that gradually picked up speed until the room and everything around it turned to white. It was blinding. Intensifying and burning. Physically burning. *Did something go wrong?* I could feel Ryn's hand gripping my upper arm and that was the last thing I remembered before crumbling to the ground and spinning wildly in a vortex that was void of light and sound.

When I finally opened my eyes, everything around me was blurry and the ground felt wet and marshy. As my eyes gradually regained focus, I could see that we were probably in the outskirts of the city. Low-lying brush and some tall, thin pine trees seemed to stretch everywhere. I kept scanning the horizon for power lines but didn't spot any. I stood up slowly and started to wipe the caked-on mud off of my jeans. *Oh no. We should have at least tried to dress for the right time period.* Ryn was just a few feet away but pre-occupied looking at something.

I shouted to him about the clothing but he kept screaming at me to stay still.

"What are you making such a big fuss about? What's the big—?" And then, I realized that I had been right all along. Something did go horribly wrong. We moved back so far in time that we could actually feel the friction.

"Oh my God, Ryn! It's a mastodon! And for the life of me, I can't remember if they're carnivores."

"No, they're not, but we could get crushed under its feet. Just stay still and let it pass."

I held my breath and tried to stop my body from shaking. *It'll be OK. It'll be OK. Time will right itself.*

The creature cruised slowly through the brush, nibbling at the taller trees before it finally lumbered out of our sight.

"I don't understand this, Ryn. No one bumped into us and the beam of light was relatively short. We should only have gone back decades. Not geological eras! Something must have jolted that time-space continuum."

And then it dawned on me. Ryn kept losing his text messages with Linna and my mom complained about solar flare interference earlier in the week. But before I could say anything, Ryn had figured it out, too.

"Crap! I bet it was those stupid sunspots. They must interfere somehow with the laws of refraction. How long did Mom say they were going to last?"

"Just a few days."

"Well, let's just hope a few days in our time are a few days in this one because that mastodon isn't the creature we need to be worried about. If

I remember correctly, wasn't this the era of the saber-tooth tiger? And those things are carnivores!"

I started to walk towards Ryn when I heard a soft scraping noise coming from the bushes near us and froze. My throat tightened and my fingers began to tremble. Whatever was making the noise seemed to be headed our way. I could tell by the movement of the branches, even though the soft ground had muted the sound of the animal's hooves or paws. Then, it started to move faster—breaking branches and trampling through the brush.

For an instant I thought I saw something dark beige and black, but the thing moved too quickly and when I finally saw what it was, it frightened me more than any prehistoric beast ever would.

Chapter Four:
Ryn

I had to admit, Aeden was taking this a hell of lot better than I thought she would. I mean, of all the rotten times in history, we had to wind up somewhere in the stinkin' Ice Age. Well, it's a damn nightmare if you ask me. And I know what's coming. I had to sit through "The Dawn of Civilization" in my sixth grade social studies class. It was the worst 45 minutes of my life! How on earth were we were going to survive this for the next few hours, let alone days?

Every sound set off an alarm in my body and when I heard the rustling coming from the bushes, I froze. Whoever the idiot was who said that early man had two choices—fight or flight, was dead wrong. He forgot the third—freeze. Because that's exactly what I did. Then, I got a good look at what was causing the noise, but before I could say anything, Aeden was shouting at the top of her lungs.

"AJAY! AJAY! It's you!"

"Of course it's me. What the hell happened? Don't answer, because I already know. We've been kidnapped. Drugged. Drugged and kidnapped. Oh my God! Where the hell are we?

This is some miserable swamp. I don't recognize anything. Oh my God! Whoever drugged us must have kidnapped us and driven us all the way to Louisiana. At least I think this is Louisiana... I mean, with all the swamps and yuck! And my bag! I don't have my bag. They must have stolen it. My cell phone's in it. Do you have yours? Call 911. Call the police! Call the state troopers! Oh my God, don't just stand there looking at me, Aeden, call the damn police!"

Ajay kept screaming about being kidnapped and muttered something about her nails looking even worse. I shot Aeden a glance and shrugged my shoulders. Of all the harrowing creatures that we could encounter in this era, it had to be Ajay! I was used to my sister getting all emotional and weird over something, but compared to the ranting that was taking place a few feet from me, Aeden's meltdowns were nothing. I had to step in.

"Calm down, Ajay. Get a grip. You weren't kidnapped. You weren't drugged."

"Then what? What? WHAT happened?"

I'm not really good at dealing with hysterical people. I don't even like it when babies start crying. But I had to do something. I grabbed both of Ajay's wrists and forced her to look straight at me. Then, I took a quick breath and spoke quietly.

"Don't start screaming, whatever you do. Just listen and tell me the last thing you remember."

Ajay rolled her eyes and started a new tirade.

"The appointments were running late in the nail salon so I ran into 'The Sun Catcher.' I could see both of you going in there. I had to squint because the sunlight was bouncing off of the little glass nick-knacks. You and Aeden were looking at something, and just as I was about to speak, I felt really dizzy and weird. Then, the colors started spinning around and I couldn't even feel my own body. Honestly, I think we were drugged. Someone must have sprayed something in the air. When I got up, I was here. Filthy from being dumped in a swamp! And you're telling me it didn't happen!"

Aeden moved in closer and spoke softly.

"What Ryn's about to tell you is going to freak you out, but don't let it. You'll be OK."

"I'll be OK? I'll be OK if you call 911!"

"Ajay," Aeden continued, "we don't have our cell phones either, and even if we did, it wouldn't help."

"Get a grip, Ajay," I said as I let go of her wrists. "What happened to us was a natural phenomenon. It was time displacement. Those solar flares must have interfered with the time-space continuum. Somehow the sunlight and all that glass got electrically charged by the flares.

So…we're kind of in a different era. Same place, I think, but a different era."

"Then do something!" Ajay started screaming. "Do something right now and get us back! I mean it, Ryn! DO SOMETHING NOW! I WANT TO GET OUT OF HERE NOW!"

"He's not the freaking Wizard of Oz, Ajay," Aeden yelled. "And you're not Dorothy, so deal with it!"

Ajay stopped screaming for just a second and started to look around. Then, she got really, really quiet, and I almost wished she would have kept screaming. I shook her shoulder and waited for a response. Nothing.

"Say something, Ajay. Are you all right?"

"No, I'm not all right. I'm not all right because I've seen this place before. The ferny leaves, the swamp water, the way the mist hangs over the air. You know where I've seen this place? I'll tell you where! It's in a painting at the historical museum in the pre-historic section! Missouri had dinosaurs, you know. Dinosaurs. We're dead. Oh my God!"

I let out a slow breath and enunciated each word as if I were talking to a three year old.

"There are no dinosaurs in this era."

Ajay stared at me, emotionless and I continued.

"It's a later era. You know, the one with the Woolly Mammoths. We'll be fine if we just stay out of their way."

I had no intention of giving Ajay a lesson on the Pleistocene epoch because that would have meant mentioning giant grizzly bears, wild boars and my personal favorite, the saber-tooth tiger. I just needed her to stay calm long enough for us to figure out where we could wait out this blasted time ripple without getting ourselves killed. I'm all for the eco-system, but not when I'm the main meal.

"We need to find a better shelter than this spot near the water. Let's start walking quietly and look for craggy rocks with an overhead. But steer clear of caves."

The last thing I needed was for Ajay to get Aeden all worked up. And I didn't want either of them to find out how freaking scared I was. I had a right to be scared out of my gourd! It was going to be nightfall in a few hours and then what? Dinner by the campfire? I could feel my tongue pressing against my front teeth. Fire! We need to figure out how to start a fire. It would be the only thing that could protect us. My mind started racing. *Flint gets rubbed against steel. There's no steel. It wasn't invented. I don't carry matches. I don't smoke. Maybe I should have taken that cigarette from Gary Griffin in the 7th grade. I'd have a pocket full of matches by now or my own personal lighter. Don't need a lighter. Just a magnifying glass. Who the hell walks around with a magnifying glass? Rub two sticks together. Does that really work? Where has that ever worked?* I couldn't seem to shut my mind off. But Aeden's shriek sure as hell managed to do that for me.

"They're coming toward us! Look at them! There must be 10 or 11 of them! They look so cute!"

"They're wild boars, Aeden, and they're not cute! They're omnivores and maybe they got sick of the salad bar and are ready for the entree. Quick! We've got to scramble up the nearest trees. Start climbing! I'm going to help Ajay!"

Out of the corner of my eye, I could see my sister grabbing the spiky limbs from one of those pine trees. I reached over to give Ajay a boost, but before I could do anything, she was scrambling up that tree as if she had done it a million times before. By now, the boars were just a few feet from us. I had no time to find my own tree.

"Move quicker, Ajay, I've got to climb up this one, too!"

"My arms are getting scratched, Ryn. These stupid branches are all prickly. It's bad enough my nails are ruined, now my arms are a mess!"

"Just keep climbing. No one gives a crap about your nails."

Then I could hear Ajay sniffling and I shook my head. Last thing I needed was for her to lose it again. So I tried to say something comforting.

"The wild boars don't care if your nails are polished. OK?"

For some reason, that only made things worse. Ajay started hyperventilating and Aeden began yelling at me for being insensitive.

"Insensitive, Aeden? Insensitive? Really? You're worried about that? How about the fact that at any minute some starving beast can leap out of nowhere and sink its eight inch long canines into us?"

Just then, Ajay let out a scream that lingered long enough in the air to hurt my ears.

"I'm just exaggerating, Ajay. Calm down!"

"Well, I'm not, look down. LOOK DOWN, RYN!"

This was worse than one of those horror movies where they say, "Don't go in the cellar. Don't go in the cellar," but the brainless girl always does. I shouldn't have looked down. I shouldn't have looked down, because the image I saw will be giving me nightmares for the rest of my life. I'll be forty years old and in psychoanalysis to get over this one.

Below us, a giant bear with a short face was tearing into one of those boars with such force that I could actually hear the bones breaking in the poor animal's back. Blood was everywhere. The other boars had scattered and the area around us had gotten deathly quiet.

All I could think of was how strong that bear's teeth must have been in order to slash open the hide of the boar and crush its bones. *Please don't look up, whatever you do. Don't look up. Just eat the boar. There's plenty of meat on the boar. DO NOT LOOK UP. DO NOT LOOK UP AND SEE US.*

Suddenly, I heard the sharp sound of a branch breaking and looked over to see that Aeden had lost her hold on the tree. She was slipping down fast. Too fast. And there was nothing any of us could do to stop her from falling. Every part of me felt numb as I watched her sliding toward certain death. I had to do something. Anything. I bent my knees, yelled as loud as I could and jumped with enough force to expect a really painful landing on the ground. And I was right.

My body felt as if it were being torn into pieces. Devoured into chucks of skin and muscle. Everything burned. And the world started to spin around me so quickly that I found myself gagging on my own saliva. And then, I felt as if someone had dropped an anvil on my chest. It was impossible for me to get air. Impossible for me to move. I swear I could see the air turning red as everything around me began to fade.

Chapter Five:
Ajay

I knew I was hallucinating because that's the only logical explanation. I *was* drugged. Someone must have drugged me and until it wears off, I'm living this nightmare with imaginary Ryn and Aeden while the real Ryn and Aeden probably think I'm still in the nail salon. They have no idea what happened to me. *Who the heck would want to drug me? Kidnap me?* I always thought hallucinations would be colorful weird things like the caterpillar in *Alice and Wonderland*, not some grizzly ten-foot tall bear tearing into hairy pigs and chewing up their bones.

But it's real to me. Real for now. And real scary. I heard the branch break on Aeden's tree just as Ryn yelled like a wild man. I couldn't bring myself to look down. *How can these awful visions be floating around in my mind? I don't even go to scary movies!* I closed my eyes and held on to the narrow tree trunk. *I am personally going to see to it, that whoever did this to me, gets arrested and put away for life. Life! I mean it.*

I knew Aeden had fallen right on top of the bloody boar, inches from the bear's mouth. And Ryn jumped, too. I couldn't look. Even though I knew it wasn't real, it was still terrifying and it only got worse.

The air around me got heavier and it was harder to breathe. *Oh my God, they're probably trying to kill me. To suffocate me!* I was taking deep breaths, fighting off the maniac who was doing this to me. But it became harder and harder until I got so dizzy that I let go of the tree. But instead of falling, I was spinning. Spinning in all directions. I only opened my eyes once, and that's when I saw the red air. Nothing but crimson red air. And then...nothing at all.

Chapter Six:
Aeden

The branch broke before I could grab another one and I landed hard—on my knees. As I lifted my head, I could see the fresh blood on the bear's mouth. Blood that stuck to its hair and coated its teeth. It lifted its head for just a second before bending down and tearing into the boar's neck and face. I could hear my brother yelling but he sounded miles away.

I placed my hands slowly on the ground, to give me enough momentum to stand, but something pushed down so hard on my back that I was face down in the muck, unable to catch my breath. *Another bear?* Then, my eyes started to burn and it felt as if dust was everywhere. Red dust. Strange, rancid smelling red dust. Bright flashes of light seemed to come out of nowhere and I could feel the dust clinging to my body. Soft at first, but then heavier, thicker. I was being buried alive. And I couldn't move. The more I struggled to get up, the force that had me pinned got tighter. My skin began to burn and I felt an odd metallic taste in my mouth.

And that was the last thing I remembered before time slipped again.

Chapter Seven: Ryn

The pain in my chest was nothing compared to the stabbing pain in my ears. *If I wind up losing my hearing over this, I am going to be really pissed!* I was still on the ground but the air smelled like smoke and exhaust. And the sounds were different, too. Crunching sounds, like gravel under car tires. The sunlight was blinding and all I could do was lay on my side, squinting. Another crunching sound and more exhaust fumes. The burning and stinging I felt on my body wasn't my skin being torn off by the bear. Guess that was supposed to be the good news. The bad news was the fact that it was the force of time, flinging me ahead. So far in the future from the Pleistocene epoch, that it actually hurt. But not as much as Ajay standing over me and screaming at the top of her lungs.

"Now where the hell are we, Ryn? Aeden has no clue. She's over there by the road, trying to look for you."

Then, before I could do anything, Ajay yelled for my sister.

"He's over here, Aeden. By this big rock pile!"

By now I was standing and trying to get the dust and small pieces of rock out of my hair. A dirt road was just a few feet ahead. As Aeden walked toward me, Ajay continued bellowing and whining.

"My new jeans are torn in all the wrong places! And my hair is a mess! I'll need hours in the salon just to look normal. We've got to get out of here and get home! I still think we were all drugged. We had to have been drugged. Did you guys see the giant bear eating the pigs or was that just something in my mind? I feel better now. It was just a hallucination. Just wait till my parents find out who did this to me! I'm going over to the road to wave a car down. We must really be in the boonies. It's a dirt road of all things!"

I grabbed Ajay by the sleeve of her shirt and she tumbled forward.

"I almost fell, Ryn. What's wrong with you?"

"I tried to tell you before, Ajay, you're not imagining this. We're really rippling through time. It happens. Something about light and solar flares. Just because you see a dirt road, it doesn't mean we're in the 21st century. We need to figure out where we are and then what we're going to do."

"I'll tell you what I'm going to do. I'm going to flag a car down because you're nuts!"

"Ajay, don't!" Aeden screamed, but it was too late. The driver in the yellow and white Chevy pulled off the road and rolled down his window. A song I had never heard was playing on the radio. *Oh, now lawdy, lawdy, lawdy Miss Clawdy, girl you sure look good to me.*

I only got to hear the first few lyrics because Ajay had a complete and total meltdown at the expense of the driver.

"Oh my God! Oh my God! You've got to get me out of here! I swear, it's not safe. Someone kidnapped me—tossed me in a festering swamp. But that's not the worst part. Whatever they did, it made me hallucinate. Have you ever hallucinated? Well, it's horrible. I mean it. Ugly boars being eaten by a giant bear and then the awful air turning red—"

All I could think of was that she was going to get us locked up or taken to some mid-century hospital for a psych evaluation. And they believed in shock treatments back then! Crap! *Keep your mouth shut, Ajay. Keep your big mouth shut!* But before I could say or do anything, the guy started laughing hysterically.

"Whoa—you kids from the Theater Playhouse are really hams! If you want a ride back to the place, all you have to do is ask! By the way, are those the lines from some new play? I bet it's a comedy!"

Just as Ajay was about to open her mouth again, I raced over to the car window and leaned in.

"Yeah, we're from the Theater Playhouse. Can you give us a ride back?"

"Sure, hop in. Every summer it's the same thing. You kids from The Playhouse just can't resist poking around in *Peccary Pit.*"

"Peccary Pit?"

"That's what the locals call this place. So, did you find any good fossils? Lots of dead boar remains down in there and who knows what else."

Then he looked closely at Ajay and my sister.

"Boy, you ladies are covered in dirt and your dungarees are all rolled down. Must have been doing a lot of digging."

"Dungawhat?" Ajay blurted out just as Aeden gave her a quick kick and pointed to their jeans.

"Yeah, Ajay," I added quickly. "Your clothes are a mess, better get in the car so we can go back and change."

Ajay was about to say something when Aeden gave her a nudge. As I sat down and slammed the door to the front passenger side, I could see that Ajay was fiddling around looking for a seatbelt. *Damn it, Ajay. Seatbelts won't be used until the 1960s. Quit looking for one.*

By now the car was back on the dirt road, heading to some playhouse. At least we had a destination and it was in the 20th century.

The song on the radio just ended and the DJ started in.

"You've just been listening to 'Lawdy Miss Clawdy,' putting Lloyd Price on the top of the charts for the year. Yes- sir-ee, that song's going to make 1952 famous. What a great year we're in. Stay tuned for more top 10 songs, but first, a word from our sponsor, Excelsior Mineral Springs Water, the only water that cures all ailments."

If I could have shoved a giant apple in her mouth, or anything for that matter, I would have. Ajay was becoming a liability and there was no way to stop her.

"I love those oldie stations! Do you have Sirius Radio?"

"I don't know if I'd call it serious," the guy in the red checkered shirt said. "Those DJ's are usually playing jokes or just horsing around."

Just then, he pulled off the road to a wide tree-lined path. The sign in front looked as if it could use a paintjob.

Mark Twain Summer Theater Playhouse

"We'll walk up the path. Thanks so much for the ride," Aeden said as she opened the door and got out. I was already standing off to the side, ready to yank Ajay out and start walking before she decided to ask the guy anything else.

"Thanks again," I muttered.

"You're welcome. Hope you have a good season. My wife and I try to get to a play each summer, but it's not always easy with two young kids at home. By the way, my name's Hank Clayton and I'm a surveyor with the state transportation department. Well, at least I was. Got appointed to the state highway commission. Right now I'm juggling two jobs but not for long. Anyway, I'll be looking for you on stage!"

Before I could say anything, he rolled up the window and took off. That's when Ajay started up again. Only this time, I really paid attention.

"That is SO weird. My great-grandfather's name was Hank Clayton and he had two children. Do you think that guy's a relative of mine?"

Aeden's mouth widened and I could tell by the look on her face that we had really messed up this time. Worse yet, Ajay had no clue that it was 1952. My parents always used the expression, "waiting for the other shoe to drop," but I never gave it much thought until that moment. Hell! I wasn't waiting for the other shoe to drop. I was waiting for heavy boots to come crashing down and I honestly had no idea what to do. Stupid solar flares!

Chapter Eight: Aeden

*T*he taste in my mouth was awful—like the kind you get when you have a cavity filled and all that metal and blood just swish around between your teeth and gums. Thankfully, my skin stopped burning, but my head felt heavy and dull. I was wedged among some large rocks and it took all my effort to stand up. Ryn was nowhere in sight. The only thing I could see was a dirt road. It meant we were back in civilization, or at least out of the Ice Age.

Ajay was a few yards away, partially hidden by some trees and brush. I tried to yell to her but my voice was soft and raspy. Whatever effects the time travel ripple may have had on her, one thing was certain. It didn't hurt her voice.

"Hey, Aeden. Over here! Ryn's over here!"

As I started to walk over to them, I could hear Ajay complaining about her clothes and her hair. *That girl is going to drive us insane. Of all the self-centered, vain people in the world, we had to wind up with Ajay Montgomery.* I mean, my hair was a mess, too. And I had dirt under my fingernails. But gee whiz, I was almost eaten by some sort of prehistoric bear. Next to that, I didn't give a hoot about how much dirt I had on me!

Then all of sudden, Ajay flags down a car and demands to be taken home. It wasn't her fault. She had no idea that she was trapped in a time-space continuum. And she didn't pay attention either. If she had, she would have come to the same realization that Ryn and I did—that the driver of the car was her great-grandfather. We managed to arrive back in time before his murder.

Well, maybe it was a good thing that she didn't know. She would have wanted us to prevent his murder and we just couldn't do that. Ryn must have explained it to me a zillion times. Once the events are set in history, changing even the smallest of details would have unbelievable ramifications on the future. Still...it's like watching a burning building knowing that there are people inside and not being able to help them.

I watched as the car drove off and then looked at the sign for the Playhouse. Ajay was staring at it, too, and grumbling.

"Why on earth would that guy drop us off here and not take us to the nearest town?"

Ryn let out a slow, deliberate breath.

"Because he thinks we're part of the summer theater crew. What were we supposed to tell him, Ajay? That we're from the future?"

"You and Aeden are giving me the creeps. Seriously, just because the guy had a vintage car, doesn't mean this is 1952 like you said."

"I didn't say it, the DJ on the radio did."

"Well, it was probably just an old taped show. They do that all the time."

"Look, Ajay, in just a few minutes we're going to be inside that theater. Just do me a favor and keep your mouth shut. Listen to how the people in the theater talk. Look at what they're wearing. Watch for clues—newspapers, candy wrappers, anything! And watch for what they don't have. You won't see a single cell phone, iPod or computer. It's 1952, so freaking deal with it!"

I didn't know if Ajay was about to yell or cry, but she never got the chance. Before we headed up the path, someone was walking straight toward us. The girl looked to be in her late teens or maybe even early twenties with her long brown hair pulled back into a ponytail and short straight bangs cut just above her eyebrows. Her jeans were rolled up and she was wearing a button down white shirt and red canvas sneakers.

"You must be the new crew members! We've been expecting you. Thought you'd call from the

Greyhound Station in Springfield for a ride. Gosh, what happened to you? Must have been a heck of a ride. Where are your things? Oh no, don't tell me you had them ship a trunk for you. The last crew that did that didn't get their things until the end of the summer. Well, don't worry—there's lots of extra clothes in the bunks. Happens all the time. Welcome to the theater! Did I mention my name? I'm Marcy. Marcy Meadows. Assistant director and actress."

Before I could say anything, Marcy kept talking.

"Actually, my real name is Marsha...well, never mind my last name, my stage name is Marcy Meadows. Sounds so theatrical, doesn't it? I mean, who wants to see a show staring plain old Marsha? So, what part of the crew did you sign up for—construction, sewing, prop making, or are you just going to be helping Edna prepare the meals?"

I don't know what came over me, but all of sudden I wanted to be on stage with Marcy Meadows.

"I can act," I said. "And sing. And dance, too. Are there any acting parts?"

A quick elbow jabbed me in the arm and Ryn spoke.

"My sister's just kidding. She'd love to work in the kitchen."

"That's terrific. I'm going to run ahead and let everyone know you're here. Oops—almost forgot. What are your names?"

Our names were unusual in the 21st century. In the 20th century, they would be just plain weird. I didn't know what to do, but Ryn thought fast.

"I'm Ryan, this is my sister Eden and our friend A J—short for Audrey Jane."

"WHAT?" Ajay said.

"She'd rather be called A J. Hates Audrey Jane!" Ryn said.

"Okey, Dokey! See you at the Playhouse. I've got to run back there fast! We're two weeks into rehearsal already."

"Audrey Jane! Audrey Jane! What the hell is the matter with you, Ryn?"

Ajay was now on a tear. No matter what my brother said, or how diplomatic he tried to be, it was useless. But I knew that the minute Ajay would step foot in the building, she'd get the shock of her life. I only hoped she'd do it quietly.

Chapter Nine:
Ryn

What a freaking nightmare! I watched as Marcy-Marsha Whoever jogged back to the Playhouse before I grabbed Aeden by both shoulders.

"What were you thinking? Have you gone totally insane? You want to act? Well, I've got news for you, Aeden, this isn't your debut into the theater world. Save it for that stupid calla lily play when we get back to Portland. *IF* we get back to Portland! We need to keep a low profile. You should know that by now. Just try to fit in so no one gets suspicious."

"The play happens to be 'Stage Door' and it's famous."

"I don't give a rat's tail if it's 'Stagecoach,' or 'Stagehand.' The point is, we need to blend into their world and that's not going to happen if you decide to become Miss Prima Donna Center Stage! Cut it out, Aeden!"

"You just want to see me wash dishes!"

"That's right Aeden. I got up this morning and said to myself, 'Gee, what can I do to make sure my sister washes dishes?' Come on, it's bad enough we've got to deal with Ajay!"

The minute I said that, I wished I had gagged on my words. Ajay spun around and lit into me like a wasp whose nest was being attached.

"Deal with me? Deal with me? What's that supposed to mean?"

"Nothing, Ajay. I just meant that it's hard enough convincing you that we're really not in our own time. But you'll see as soon as we get to the Playhouse."

"If you're right, Ryn, and I'm not saying you are, then that means the guy in the car was really my great-grandfather."

And there it was. The shoe dropped. Loud and clear. I knew what was coming next before the words even left Ajay's mouth.

"If this is 1952, then it's before my great-grandfather was murdered. We can stop his murder. We need to do that. Oh my God, Ryn. We need to find out where he was headed, where he lives, who wants to kill him. Oh my God, maybe we should call the police. We need to do something. Hurry up, I'm going to run to the Playhouse and find a phone!"

"NO!" I yelled as I tried to block her. Aeden stepped in, too, and motioned with her hands for Ajay to calm down.

"Okay, Ajay, just listen for a second. First of all, if you tell the authorities that someone is about to be murdered, you need some sort of proof. And telling them that you came here from the future isn't going to help. Get it? They'll think you're a nutcase. A certifiable nutcase. But that's not the worst thing. The worst thing is that…"

Aeden' s voice started to crack and I just blurted out the rest.

"You can't change what already happened. It's like gravity or velocity, or centrifugal force…events that happened in the past cannot be changed. I'm sorry Ajay. It is what it is. Or was, in this case. The only thing we can do is find out who did it."

"No! I'm not going to sit back and do nothing. I'm going to do everything I can to make sure my great-grandfather doesn't wind up a petrified mummy with a bullet in his head half a century later!"

I could feel the tension building in my muscles and my head started to pound. I swear, that mastodon and all the wild boars were beginning to look good to me.

"Ajay, it's really quite simple. We can't change the events in the past because if we change one thing, no matter how small or insignificant it may be, we'll wind up changing a million other things and who the hell knows what that will be like? Our whole world could be different when we get back. We just can't do it."

Then Aeden took a step towards me and whispered so that Ajay couldn't hear her.

"What about Monsieur Chastain? We made sure to keep him alive."

I responded under my breath.

"That's because he was supposed to be alive. We were born. That meant he didn't die or we wouldn't exist. It's different with Ajay. You heard the guy in the car, her great-grandfather. He said that they had two young kids at home. One of them was probably Ajay's grandparent. It wouldn't matter if he was killed because the kids were already born."

"But what if....what if Ajay's great-grandfather had a third child...one who wasn't born yet?"

"He didn't. Because Ajay *was* born, and the guy's body was found decades later. It's a no brainer, Aeden. We can't go back and un-do history."

And then, a sharp screeching voice made sure that I'd never whisper again.

"Who says you can't? Screw gravity and velocity and that centrifugal thing! I want to save my great-grandfather and you can't stop me!"

Chapter Ten:
Ajay

The Playhouse reeked of musty wood and paint and the whole place looked worse than the stupid "cafetorium" in my old elementary school. A few people were moving props onto the stage and some guy was yelling for the cast. "Cast in five! Cast in five!" Someone was on a ladder adding huge stage lights to the black rod that ran across the front of the frayed red curtain. The lights were ancient! But it wasn't until I got a good look at what the people were wearing that I realized Ryn may have been right after all. And he was insistent.

"Deal with it, Ajay! Just deal with it!"

Then, Marcy-Marsha came rushing over to us and clapped her hands to get everyone's attention.

"Meet the new kids on the crew—Ryan, Eden and Audrey Jane!"

I wanted to vomit and kick Ryn in the knee but Marcy-Marsha kept talking.

"And guess what? They had their things shipped by trunk, just like the crew from last summer. So please share your spare clothes and stuff with them. If anyone's going to the drugstore in town later, pick up some extra toothbrushes and combs, OK?"

Next thing I knew, Marcy-Marsha was motioning us to a small room off to the side of the stage.

"You folks must be hungry. There's peanut butter, jelly and bread in the fridge. We had enough profits from last summer to replace an old icebox. Oh, and there's also bug juice. Help yourself. I'll be back in a few minutes to show you the bunks."

Then she took a closer look at us and gasped.

"Oh my gosh. How did you all get so scraped up? What did they do? Throw you from the bus? Don't tell me you stumbled on that old dirt road. I swear, that road is a hazard. I wish they would pave it, but that's not going to happen. The state highway commission's planning on paving another road instead. Part of its new modernization program. Well, it won't help us. In fact, it may put us out of business. Who's going to want to drive on dirt roads to see a play when they can go to one of the bigger cities for that? Oh, about your cuts...there's some mercurochrome in the first aid kit by the sink. Band-Aids, too. Help yourself. OK, I've got to get to the stage. See you in a few minutes."

As she walked out the door, I looked at Ryn and Aeden.

"What the hell is mercurochrome? It sounds nasty."

"It is," Ryn replied. "It's some kind of red liquid they used as an antiseptic. But I think there's mercury in it. Whatever you do, don't touch it! Let's just wash our cuts off in the sink."

Aeden found a few dish towels and began to wet them under the faucet as she spoke.

"Take a good look, Ajay. No paper towels. No Clorox wipes. No soft soap. Just an old bar of yucky hand soap. I'm telling you, this is 1952. And if you don't believe me, then take a good look at that calendar on the wall. The one with the Chevy on it."

Someone was crossing off the days, one by one. Six days in all, and if Aeden was right, it was July 7, 1952. I would have had a better time believing in space aliens if it weren't for the fact that everything around us was so outdated. And yet, Marcy-Marsha was acting as if this was the most modern of times. I bit my lip and sat down at the small wooden table starring at the funny plastic salt and pepper shakers.

"So now what do we do?"

Ryn handed me a damp towel and sighed.

"As long as we're stuck in this decade, we act as if we belong. Whatever you do, don't use any modern expressions and remember, they know nothing about technology. I'm not even sure if they had transistor radios or television!"

"No television? You mean we just....live?"

"For heaven's sakes, Ajay, it won't last forever. And since we're here, we've got to make it our business to find out who killed your great-grandfather."

"No, Ryn. We've got to make it our business to find out who's *going* to kill him."

"Either way, it won't be easy. Best thing we can do is to listen to what everyone is saying and try to figure out a motive. That guy, I mean, your great-grandfather, said he worked for the state highway department. That's the same department that's going to put the Playhouse out of business if they build a road elsewhere. Maybe someone in this Playhouse is responsible for his murder."

"He's not dead, yet. Ryn! So stop acting as if it's over and done with. I mean it. Help me save him. I doubt it's going to mess up the whole future of the world!"

"Ajay, I'm about to lose it. Listen carefully. You don't know and I don't know and no one in the continental United States knows what your great-grandfather would have been like if he lived. Maybe he invented something that would have changed the world. Or maybe he saved someone's life who later wound up killing hundreds of people. Anything could have happened. It didn't because he didn't live to make it happen. And that's the way it's got to be. I don't make the freaking rules of nature! I just accept them!"

"Well that's your problem, Ryn, because I don't!"

"You don't what?" Marcy-Marsha said as she came back in the room.

"I, uh, I...don't want to use any mercurochrome. I'm fine."

"Great! Come on, I'll show you the bunks. Hope you don't mind sharing them with bedbugs!"

I let out a shriek as Marcy-Marsha started laughing.

"I'm only kidding. The accommodations aren't the greatest but the only bugs you'll have to fight off are mosquitos. And everyone knows, they're harmless."

Harmless? Didn't they know about West Nile Virus? Aeden gave me one of her "keep your mouth shut" looks and I nodded. We followed Marcy-Marsha to two large cabins that stood side by side. The girls' cabin had a pink flamingo painted over the door and the boys' cabin had some sort of blue duck.

"The outhouses are behind the cabins. Use a flashlight. We have snakes and all sorts of critters. And use the buddy system. Don't go alone. Someone even saw a bear around here. Can you imagine how frightening that would be?"

"I can't even imagine," Ryn said as Aeden and I tried to keep from laughing. And that laugh would turn out to be the only one I'd have for a long, long time.

Chapter Eleven:
Aeden

I woke up in an instant and sat straight up in my bed. Something was wrong. But what? I had no idea. Just a feeling. A strong sense of dread as if I was at the bottom of a deep pit with no beginning and no end. Ajay was fast asleep in the small metal bed next to mine. An afternoon of painting backdrops and moving props must have really wiped her out. Everyone else, too, for that matter. The other 12 or 13 girls in our cabin were dead to the world. At least for the next few hours.

The windows were open and I could smell that woodsy-cedar scent mixed with a dank, earthy undertone. There was enough moonlight for me to make my way to the outhouse, but I wasn't about to go alone and there was no way I was going to wake-up Ajay. *Just hold it till morning. You're not a baby.*

As I tried to find a comfortable position, I couldn't rid myself of the overwhelming premonition that something terrible was about to happen, or already had. In spite of the heavy woolen blanket on my bed, my body was getting those prickly bumps that indicated one thing. I was scared. Scared with no rational reason. I'd been in worse situations before. Yet this time, something was really off. And the more frightened I became, the more I needed to use the outhouse. *Try not to think about it. Get it out of your mind.* And then, I heard the rustling sound of feet crunching on twigs. Someone was just outside of the cabin. I pulled the blanket over my head and tried to breathe quietly. More feet. More crunching. How many people were out there? *Calm down. Someone probably got up before you and is coming back from the stupid outhouse. Stop being such a baby.* And then, they spoke. Softly, but audible enough for me to hear every word. But the night air distorted the voices. Two men or was it a man and a woman?

"Are you crazy? Hiding a gun. Why did you agree to do that?"

"I owed a favor."

"But a gun?"

"It's just for a little while."

"Where did you put it?"

"Don't worry. No one's going to find it. No one's going to be driving tonight. I've got to get back. Shh..."

"I just hope you know what you're doing."

Then, the sound of more branches crunching and the voices faded away. My mind had made the jump from dread to panic. Then, I thought of something and started to let out a slow breath. *It was probably two cast members rehearsing their lines. That's what it was. Two people rehearsing for one of the plays. But in the middle of the night? Well, maybe they couldn't sleep. That had to be it. They were just running lines for a play.* But then, I realized something. None of the summer plays had anything to do with guns. I know. I saw the lists posted by the stage door. "The Merry Wives of Windsor." That's Shakespeare. No guns. "The Glass Menagerie." Tennessee Williams. Depressing, but no guns. And finally, the musical "Brigadoon." I could have had a great part in that play if Ryn wasn't so insistent that I just do stage work!

Ryn! The moment I thought about him I knew that's where my sense of foreboding came from. It was crazy. Ludicrous really. He was probably sound asleep in his bunk, all worn out from building stage sets. I could hear him complaining when he thought he was alone.

"This would be done by now if I had power tools! How do these people stand it?"

More than anything, I wanted to walk over to his bunk and make sure he was still there. But where was he going to be? I mean, if Ajay and I were still here, then that would mean Ryn was, too. At least that's what I thought. Then why did I have the most awful feeling that he was in danger? *It's just your imagination. Exhaustion, dealing with Ajay and flipping through time. Get some sleep. It's all in your head.*

Unfortunately, it wasn't. And there was nothing I could do about it.

Chapter Twelve: Ryn

My neck was killing me and the sharp stabs from whatever bird's feathers were stuffed inside my pillow weren't helping. How did people sleep like this? It'll be decades until someone invents Memory Foam. Another week of this and my neck might have permanent damage. I tried every sort of position and kept scrunching the pillow until I finally got it to stop torturing me. The hellish day I had was bad enough.

When this is all over, I will never build theater sets again. Never! My guidance counselor can add that to the list of careers that I will avoid. My arms were aching and my legs were all cramped from bending over. Still, I was able to pound enough nails and saw enough plywood to get the first scene of "Brigadoon" done. *How many crappy scenes are there? I should have asked Aeden.* At least we had a place to stay and some food. If you call a slice of meatloaf and a spoonful of beans a meal. I guess when you think about it, my sister had the worst end of it. She had to keep an eye on Ajay. I tried to explain that our best bet would be some simple detective work. Hell, I've seen enough shows. You don't have to be the "Mentalist" or that "Psych" guy to listen to what's going on and ask questions.

We just needed to find out who would want to kill some guy who worked for the state transportation department. And, we could do a heck of a lot of listening when the plays start running and the theater fills up. People in the audience talk. Yeah, it sounds callous and cold, but it's what happened. The guy was killed. Murdered. Even if we just met him. And if it hasn't happened yet, it will.

I figured out that if I kept my head really still, I wouldn't feel the feathers pinching into my skin. At least I had a sheet between me and the wool blanket, otherwise it would have been double torture. Who knows how long I stayed in that position, but it finally worked. I could feel myself drifting off. Everyone else in my bunk had beaten me to it. I could hear guys snoring, snorting and farting under their covers. I made a mental note to remind myself not to get a college roommate. If the noise wasn't bad enough, the odor was. Still, I was too tired to think about it. I just kept nodding off. Deeper and deeper until time and sleep collided.

But the odor got more pungent and I couldn't stand it. I knew I'd have to get up and open a window. Maybe all of them. And my pillow. It had gotten worse. Those feathers felt as if they were barbs from a rose bush. As I started to sit up, I could feel some sort of hot breath near my face. Stinky breath. Some kid really needed to get acquainted with mouthwash. And who the heck would be bothering me in the middle of the night?

My voice was low and creaky and I hadn't opened my eyes yet. "What's the matter? What do you want?"

The kid didn't say a word, but by now, I could smell his body, too, and it had the most awful stench. *Don't these people use a shower? It's 1952, not the Dark Ages.* Then, I opened my eyes and wished I hadn't. It wasn't a kid standing near my bed. And worse yet, I wasn't in my bed. I was lying on the ground in the dark, my head tangled in a pile of twigs, leaves and rocks. *Don't tell me I was sleepwalking. This is what you get for doing construction work. You wind up exhausted and sleepwalking with some stupid raccoon near you.* But it wasn't a raccoon. It wasn't any animal from the 21st century. No raccoon had eyes like that.

By now, I was wide awake and in full panic mode. The moonlight was bright enough for me to see that the creature standing over my body was a giant ground sloth. Time tripped and I had lunged back to the Ice Age. *Pull it together, Ryn. Sloths are herbivores. It won't eat you. Then why the hell is it smelling me?* Then I remembered a scene from that movie they showed us in school. Sloths were eating the dead bodies of animals that the saber-tooth tigers killed. *It's checking me out because it thinks I'm dead.*

Slowly, I reached back and moved my right arm above my head and felt the ground for a rock. It needed to be a big rock. Nothing. Just smaller stones. Then, I tried my left hand and was able to grasp a decent size weapon. *I'll have to be quick. I'll need to sit up, throw the rock at the sloth's head and then run as fast as I can.* I tried not to think about the fact that I would be running barefooted. I just needed to be running.

My body acted automatically. Good thing, too, because cognitively may have been too late. I scrambled myself up from the ground, threw the rock and screamed. Whoever said that sloths move slowly was wrong. Dead wrong. The thing took after me like a coyote who had just spied a rabbit. No time to think about the soles of my feet. I scurried through the brush and wove around the small trees hoping the thing would lose interest. It didn't. I could hear it, lumbering behind me. But there was something else. A new sound. Faster. Lighter. It followed us as I kept pushing myself forward. And then, I heard a crashing sound as if every tree was falling to the ground. With a quick glance backwards, I saw the sloth stumble over itself as the sharp teeth from a saber-tooth tiger plunged into the poor beast's neck. A lump formed in my throat as I listened to the whimpering sound that the dying creature made.

Just run, Ryn. Run. Run like there's no tomorrow.

The moon had moved in the sky and it was almost dawn. I was safe for a few minutes. Still, I held a sharp rock in my hand, just in case. But my body was getting tired. Exhausted. I stopped near a small boulder and sank down to the ground, closing my eyes for just a second. And then, an ear-splitting sound reverberated in my head until I felt as if I was going to heave. It jolted me awake and I tightened the grip on the rock.

It was daylight and I was lying on my back, a few yards from the bunk. I could see some people making their way to the outhouse. Time flipped again. Or had I been sleepwalking? I looked carefully at the rock I was holding. It didn't look like anything I'd seen before. And the bottoms of my feet were raw and burning. Large cuts. Bloody cuts. I knew where I had been and the worst part of it was, I knew I was going back. Time had become unstable.

I held the rock as I made my way back to the cabin. More people were headed to the outhouse. And they noticed my bare feet.

"Boy, Ryan, you must have been in one heck of a hurry to get to the latrine. No one goes there without shoes! You were lucky you didn't get bitten by something."

"Yeah, I was lucky all right," I said, just as I heard Aeden calling out my name. She was out of breath and running faster than I'd seen her run in a long time.

"Ryn! I knocked on your cabin but you weren't there. Ajay's missing! She must have slipped out last night. Used her pillow and a rumpled up blanket to make it look like she was still in the bed. Oh my God, Ryn! She's run off!"

Chapter Thirteen:
Aeden

I've never liked babysitting. But having to keep tabs on someone my own age was much worse. So why should I feel guilty about losing Ajay? Did Ryn really expect me to stay awake all night just in case she decided to do something stupid? Still...I felt guilty. Guilty and annoyed. But that was before I found out what happened to my brother.

"Oh my God, Ryn! You mean to tell me that you got twisted back to the Ice Age? What if the same thing happened to Ajay? She could be there right now. Running for her life. Or...or..."

"I don't think so, Aeden. The time loop was much more localized than that. I mean, it only grabbed me. You were just a few feet away from her and nothing happened to you. We've got to figure that she ran off. And I bet I know why and where. She's trying to warn her great-grandfather about his murder."

"It was the middle of the night, Ryn. What was she going to do? Hitch a ride on a dirt road? Even Ajay's too smart for that."

"Look, before we go crazy jumping to conclusions, let's just try to look for her around here. And let's hope she turns up before the director and playhouse manager get involved. That's all we need."

I nodded as I watched Ryn hobble back to his cabin. Then, all of sudden he yelled out.

"Hey, Aeden! I think we all should start sleeping with our shoes on. I mean it!"

It was hard to figure what freaked me out more—the thought of Ajay missing or the realization that the time-space continuum was unstable where the three of us were concerned. We didn't belong in this decade but the loop seemed to be entwined with the Ice Age. I was so deep in my thoughts that I literally bumped into two girls who were on their way back from the shower.

"Eden, right?"

"Yeah."

"That other girl, what's her name? Audrey something...Well, anyway, she's been looking for you."

"For me? She's looking for me?"

I was incredulous. It was just like Ajay to do something really stupid and then act all innocent and nonchalant about it. As if I was the person who had gone missing. I took a step closer to the girls.

"You said Audrey Jane is looking for me? Where is she? Where did she go?"

The taller of the two girls fiddled with her braids as she spoke.

"She was headed to the kitchen. Coffee's on. I'd grab my cup outside, unless of course you don't mind the cigarette smoke."

"Thanks. I'll go look for her. And yuck, I hate cigarette smoke."

"Better get used to it. Everyone in the theater smokes. Heck, half the cast and most of the crew have their own lighters. Besides, you don't believe that nonsense about smoking stunting your growth. My mother tried to scare me with that one, but it didn't work. Anyway, smoking's allowed in the kitchen but not on the set. Too worried that a lit cigarette will set the whole place on fire. Gotta hurry. Hope you find that Audrey girl."

"Thanks," I said as I raced to the cabin for a toothbrush and the change of clothes that someone had left me. *I will personally hurl Ajay back to the Ice Age when I get my hands on her!*

As it turned out, Ryn beat me to it. Not the hurling part, just finding Ajay. Ajay stuffing her face with donuts and coffee as he walked into the kitchen. I arrived a few seconds behind him. Thankfully, the other cast and crew members were heading out so no one heard us. When Ryn gets ticked, his voice gets really loud. And Ajay's apparently, gets really shrill. It was like watching "The Jerry Springer Show."

"Where did you go last night, Ajay? And don't tell me you didn't go sneaking off somewhere because I know you did."

"Aeden just had to tattle, didn't she? Just like elementary school. Well, if you must know, I thought I'd sneak out to warn my great-grandfather."

"What did you plan on doing? Walk down a dark dirt road for miles until you got to the nearest town? Hitch? Are you nuts?"

"As a matter of fact, I figured a way to drive myself to town. They've got a truck that they use for hauling stage material and props. And the key is on a small nail by the kitchen door. I figured I could locate Hank Clayton from the phonebook in the kitchen. Then, I'd drive over, tell him and be back with the truck before morning."

"Just like that. Knock on someone's door. Tell them you're from the future. Tell them someone's going to kill them and then drive off. That's a really well thought out plan! Again, Ajay, are you nuts? I'm surprised he didn't sic the local sheriff on you."

"That's because I never got very far. Stupid old truck is a standard shift. I just couldn't get it going. I know you've got to step on that clutch thing, but I couldn't figure out when and the damn thing kept stalling. I was lucky to get it back in the driveway."

"Serves you right."

"Maybe so, but I found out something that may tell us who's after my great-grandfather. See for yourself."

Ajay reached into her pocket and handed Ryn a bullet.

"Take a look. I found this in the glove compartment when I was trying to find the manual to figure out how to work that idiotic clutch. And this bullet wasn't the only one. There were a few of them in there."

Ryn just shook his head and tried not to laugh.

"It's a cartridge for a .38 revolver. Doesn't mean anything, Ajay. It would be like finding a jelly bean and thinking someone kidnapped the Easter Bunny!"

"But my great-grandfather was shot with a .38. That's what the coroner's report said."

"Do you have any idea how popular that gun was? The bullets in the glove compartment don't mean anything."

"Maybe not, but how do you explain this?"

It was a crumpled up flyer from the Missouri State Highway Commission. Something about a highway modernization and expansion program.

Same thing that Marcy-Marsha told us. Only someone had written over the memo with a new message:

You and your state buddies will have hell to pay first, Hank Clayton.

Ajay was tapping her foot and grinding her teeth as she waited for Ryn's response, but before he could say anything, the set director appeared out of nowhere and motioned for us to get going.

"Come on, you three. There's work to be done. Set's not going to build itself!"

"You know I'm right, Ryn," Ajay said as she ran past us to the Playhouse. "And I intend to do something about it."

I deliberately slowed down my pace so Ryn and I could speak privately. No one was near us but I still whispered.

"She may have already done that."

"What do you mean?"

"I think that glove compartment may have had a gun in it. A gun that Ajay has stashed somewhere."

Chapter Fourteen:
Ryn

What a stinkin' night and crummy morning! I honestly can't say which part of it was worse – the sloth or Ajay! At least the sloth wasn't driven to emotional outbursts. I swear, that girl's becoming a raving lunatic! Possibly a raving lunatic with a gun. I told Aeden to hurry back to her cabin and start looking all over in case Ajay really did find a gun and hide it somewhere.

"Then what am I supposed to do, Ryn? Re-hide it?"

"You'll have to. And then don't let Ajay out of your sight once you go into the Playhouse."

"What if I don't find a gun? I can't spend the whole morning looking."

"Do what you can. I'll make up some excuse for you."

Aeden ran back to the girls' bunk and I trudged along the path to the Playhouse. When I walked inside, everyone could see how exhausted I was.

"What's the matter, Ryan? Set building a little tough? Don't worry, you'll get used to it."

"When your hands start to bleed and crack, then you'll know you're doing a good job."

I walked over to the large wooden frame where I had left off yesterday and stared at it. It still needed some edging. As I reached for a hacksaw, the stage manager/set designer, Nick something-or-other, tapped me on the shoulder and handed me a keychain with a green rabbit's foot on one end and a car key on the other.

"Looks like we're going to need you to drive the truck to Percy's Lumberyard past Northview and pick up the discards. I thought Phil was going to do it but I can't seem to find him. Anyway, someone at the lumberyard will help you load it."

"The discards?"

"You know, the wood that can't be sold. They donate it to the Playhouse. Tax write- off for the lumberyard and a necessity for us. Just go right on this road until you get to County 125. Stay on that until you see a large blue sign for the lumberyard. Can't miss it."

"OK, uh...sure."

"And when you get back, pull it all the way into the driveway. Honestly, a trained chimpanzee could have parked it better than whoever drove it last. And the truck's only two years old. They'll beat it up at this rate."

Then Nick walked off. Never asked if I had a license. Never asked if I knew how to drive a truck. I wouldn't have been lying if I told him I had a driver's license, because I did. Yeah, yeah...it would be half a century or so from now, but a license is a license. And driving a stick shift... yep, I could do that in my sleep. I was the only kid in Portland who had to take his road test in the ancient family car - a 1998 Subaru Legacy standard shift. But Aeden will luck out. My folks will feel sorry for her and not force her to learn how to drive a stick. She'll get to take her road test on dad's car. *Aeden! She's still looking around for a gun. Better say something.*

"Hey, guys," I yelled. "Eden's on her way. She had an upset stomach."

I could see Ajay walking into the back of the theater near the large murals. She didn't hear me, or if she did, she chose not to say anything. Good. She can moan and groan to Aeden all morning. I walked quickly to the truck, climbed inside, put the keys in the ignition and put my foot down on the clutch. It took me a second or two to figure out the gear shift and then I was out of the driveway and heading down the dirt road.

County Road 125 wasn't a whole lot better. There were enough potholes in it to sink a small vessel. But Nick was right. It was easy to find the place.

Percy's Lumberyard sat at the end of a dirt driveway and consisted of a small shack and a larger open-framed building that stored all the decent lumber. Plywood, planks, and lots of 2 x 4's. Other piles of lumber seemed to be everywhere. A few old garbage cans were sitting in the middle of the parking lot, but apparently no one bothered to use them. Cigarette butts and bits of trash littered the area.

I shoved the keychain in my pocket and walked toward the office. The whole place was cluttered. Paper everywhere. Plastic ashtrays and old ceramic cups. A balding guy with glasses was sifting through some papers as he sat on a stool by a small desk. His ear was pressed to the phone and I didn't think he saw me. Not at first. But I heard every word he said.

"I'm telling you, Bob, if they put that damn highway across from the 125, it'll put us right out of business. Hell, we won't have cash flow, we'll have cash drip. Everyone's going to go straight on to Springfield or one of the bigger cities for their lumber. We won't be able to compete. You've got to talk some sense into that Clayton fellow. We didn't elect you to just sit by and watch the rest of us get railroaded. Feels as if we've already been run over by a train."

Then his eyes locked with mine and he paused.

"Call you back. I've got a customer."

I put the keychain in my pocket and took a step forward.

"I'm not exactly a customer. Nick from the Playhouse sent me here to pick up some discarded lumber."

"It's your lucky day, kid. There's a boatload of planks, boards and 2 x 4's behind the small shed. Hope you brought some gloves. Stuff's pretty rough."

"I'll manage," I mumbled.

"Look in the cab. I'm sure someone from that theater crew left a pair in there from last time. Got a guy working in the yard. Name's Owen. Just look around for him. He'll help you with the lumber."

I nodded and glanced back at the door.

"Thanks, I really---"

But before I could finish my sentence, he had picked up the phone and started to dial.

When I stepped out of the office, I could see that a few more trucks had arrived. At least four or five men were now loading lumber. If Owen was one of them, I'd have to wait my turn.

"Hey kid," someone yelled. "Looking for something?"

A tall, thin, curly haired guy in his mid to late twenties came toward me.

"Yeah," I said. "I'm looking for Owen. He's supposed to help me load some discarded lumber."

"Is that what you were told?"

"Sort of. Yeah."

"Well, I'm Owen and it's news to me."

"Never mind," I mumbled. "I can do it myself. Where's the discard pile?"

Owen pointed to a mound of wood that was taller than me and I let out a word under my breath that made him laugh.

"OK kid. Don't get bent out of shape. I'll give you a hand."

For the next twenty minutes we hoisted beams, planks and everything in-between. Halfway into the project, Owen stopped for a smoke.

"Want one?"

"No thanks. I'm fine."

"Suit yourself. So...you're working at the Summer Playhouse, huh?"

"Yeah. Set building."

"Hope it doesn't turn out to be your last season."

"What do you mean?"

"You know. Once the state starts construction on the new highway, it will pretty much block traffic from getting to you. Folks will just take in a movie somewhere else. Lumberyard's in the same mess. Heck, I'll probably lose my job. Lon's been trying to get our councilman to do something but that old jerk-butt is as useful as a fart in an iron lung."

"Lon's the owner?"

"Yeah, Lon Percy. This lumberyard's been in his family for years."

"No kidding. And now it might be forced to close?"

"Yep. And you know what the really crazy thing is?"

I shook my head and he went on.

"Those guys from the college are pitching a fit because they don't want the new highway to go on the other side of the 125. Seems it's going to be built over some old dinosaur bone pits or something like that. The college president himself even tried to talk some sense into the state highway commission but he might as well have been talking to a stone wall."

"Dinosaur bone pits? You mean like Peccary Pit? I've seen that place."

"Peccary Pit is nothing compared to the giant bone pits off of the 125. For the life of me, I don't know why those jerks from the state don't just build the road on the other side and connect it to the highways."

I took a deep breath and hoped Owen could answer my next question.

"Ever hear of someone named Hank Clayton?"

"You must be from out of town. Everyone's heard of Hank Clayton. He's the only guy working for that blasted highway commission that anyone will listen to. People either want him on their side or want him out of the way altogether. Commission is supposed to vote next week and Hank could make it go either way."

"You mean..."

"I mean, if I was Hank Clayton, I'd be sleeping with a gun under my pillow."

Chapter Fifteen: Aeden

I looked everywhere. Under dusty old cot mattresses, in cubbies and even in the piles of sleeping bags and blankets that were stashed all over the bunk. Nothing. Then I checked out the outhouse and the smelly floorboards underneath it. Ryn owes me big time! If Ajay did hide a gun someplace, it wasn't in our cabin. My hands were filthy from sifting through stuff but I couldn't waste any more time. I had to get over to the theater. I figured I would just rinse off my hands in the kitchen once I got there. But I never got the chance. Ajay attacked me with her ranting and moaning as soon as I stepped inside the Playhouse.

"Where have you been, Aeden? I've had to lug these murals all over the place! And look at me. I've got paint on my arms. It'll never come off."

"Get a grip, Ajay. It's just paint. Come on, let's just take a break and wash up in the kitchen. My hands are dirty, too."

No one seemed to notice us as we headed down the narrow corridor that separated the barn area from the actual stage. Behind us, the chorus was singing "Brigadoon" and practicing the dance routines. The kitchen was straight ahead but we never walked in. Loud voices were coming from there and we recognized them.

"Shh," I whispered. "It's Marcy – Marsha and that guy Phil, the one who does the special effects and the lighting."

Ajay tip-toed to the door and motioned for me to follow. The conversation going on inside the kitchen was real, not someone running lines for a play.

"What do you mean he told that Ryan kid to drive the truck? We don't even know if the kid has a license."

"I'm sure he does. He's old enough. And what's the big deal anyway? He's just going over to the lumberyard. He'll be back in a while."

"It's the principle of the thing. Nick should have checked with me first. I usually make those runs."

"You're not his boss. Maybe he needed you to stay here and do something else."

"Yeah, well he never said a word. I just hope that kid doesn't wind up wrecking the truck. Road's filled with potholes."

"You should be glad you're not the one loading up all that heavy lumber."

"Maybe. But I'm about to have a word or two with Nick. See you later."

Ajay and I made a quick dash out of the corridor and into the back of the theater before Phil left the kitchen.

"That was weird, Aeden. I mean, who gets all bent out of shape if their boss gives the hard work to someone else? I'd just say *happy day* and mind my own business."

"Could be Phil is really possessive about the truck. I wondered why I didn't see Ryn when I walked into the theater. I'll have to tell him about Phil's reaction."

"Boy, you two don't keep anything from each other, do you?"

"Not really. He'd find out anyway so why bother lying about anything. You know what I mean?"

I gave Ajay one of those *you're keeping something from me* looks, hoping she'd admit to finding and hiding a gun, but no luck. She just shrugged her shoulders and kept walking.

"I suppose they'll have us painting more sets. When's opening night anyway? Your brother said something about scoping out the audience for clues to my great- grandfather's murder. And then what? Just wait around?"

"Opening night is this weekend. They start with the musical and then do the serious play and end it with Shakespeare. At least that's what the calendar in the kitchen said. The scenery is already done for 'Brigadoon,' and there's really not much painting for 'The Glass Menagerie.' It's just living room furniture and a dining room table, I think. That's why we're working on the interior of a Tudor stage. Probably why they sent Ryn to the lumberyard. They're going to need lots of 2 x 4's to build that kind of thing."

"Thanks for the theater lesson, Aeden, but what I really want to know is---"

And then Ajay's voice dropped off for just a second. Long enough for me to feel a cold burning sensation in my nose.

"Something's not right, Ajay," I said as I inched closer to her, remembering what Ryn had said about staying near each other just in case.

"You feel it too? It's like the air around us is changing."

"Not just the air. Listen. They've stopped singing. I mean, we're still in the theater, but I'm not sure *when*."

I was about to take a step forward to catch a glimpse of the stage when everything around me seemed to get wavy, like those images in a funhouse mirror.

"It's happening, Aeden! Oh my God, it's happening again. I can't even stand up."

"Hold on to my arm, Ajay. It'll pass. Just stay still."

Ajay's nails bit into my wrist and that was the last sensation I felt before free-falling into nowhere.

Chapter Sixteen:
Ryn

"**H**ey Owen!" someone yelled from across the lumberyard. "These 2 x 4's ain't gonna load themselves. Quit your yakking and give us a hand!"

I looked over to see a medium built guy in his thirties or forties standing next to a stocky white-haired man who reminded me of the old guy in the Quaker Oats commercials. Both were leaning against a green Chevy pick-up that looked brand new.

"Guess you better get over there," I said as Owen turned to acknowledge them.

"Yeah, well, they can wait a second or two. Won't kill them. It's Ed Stockton and his son Tom. They own Stockton Motors in Springfield and a few restaurants up this way as well. But from the way they act, you'd think they owned all of us."

But no sooner did he start walking towards them when a light blue convertible pulled up next to him and screeched to a stop. The driver was probably younger than Owen but looked older with her blond hair all done up and heavy red lipstick on. Must have been the style.

"Owen, sweetie, I'm in a real hurry. Can you please throw eight or nine boards into the back of my car? I promised Councilman Barkley that I'd get them over to his campaign headquarters by noon and I'm running late. His committee wants to get the signs mounted and posted by tomorrow."

Before he could respond, Ed Stockton's voice shook the lumberyard.

"We don't have all day! There are other lumberyards you know, and we can take our business elsewhere."

I could see by the look on his face that Owen really wanted to help whoever that lady was in the convertible, so I did the decent thing. I stopped hoisting the discarded stuff onto the theater truck and walked over to where Ed and Tom Stockton were standing.

"I've got time. I'll give you a hand."

The older Stockton eyed me as if I had just stolen his credit card. Still, he didn't refuse my help. In a matter of minutes, Owen had finished up with the boards for the councilman and walked over to us. He didn't say a word. He just started loading the lumber until the order was complete.

"Well, that should do it gentlemen," he said as he wiped his hands on the front of his jeans and turned toward me. "I've got another order to fill."

"If you're talking about campaign signs for Councilman Barkley, no amount of lumber in the world is going to save his sorry butt. Come on, Tom. We've got business to do."

No word of thanks. Nothing. The two of them got into their truck and made sure to step on the gas hard enough to send a whirl of dirt and dust our way.

I shook my head and laughed.

"Maybe they should take their business elsewhere. What jerks!"

Owen nodded but I could tell he was holding back something.

"Jerks, yeah. But jerks with money and lots of it. This lumberyard can't afford to be choosey. Come on, I'll help you finish loading your wood."

"So," I said as I cleared the dust from my throat, "What's the deal with Councilman Barkley? Sounds like the Stocktons aren't going to be casting a vote for him."

"Councilman Barkley beat out the former councilman in the last election. That guy had been our representative for years. Lots of bad blood. Rumors, too, about corruption in the former administration but nothing anyone could prove. The Stocktons wanted their own guy in office. And they were really ticked off when

Barkley got elected. Still…they know how to strong-arm people. They'll have Barkley in their back pocket soon enough."

Just as I was about to say something, another truck pulled into the lumberyard and parked in front of the small office.

"That's Andy Pendleton. He owns a farm near here. Always needs something, but doesn't always have the means to pay. He'll work it out with Lon. Anyway, that should do it. Looks like all your discards are loaded up. It'll just take me a second to fasten them down with that old piece of rope you've got. The theater company should be happy – lots of planks and all sorts of material. It's a big pile so you'll need to use your side view mirrors. Sorry about that. Well, good luck working at the theater."

"Yeah, thanks Owen. See you again, I'm sure."

I shook his hand and got into the truck, taking my time to drive slowly out of the driveway so that I could get a good look at Andy Pendleton's truck. Something about it was familiar and then it hit me. It was an old Ford, just like the one I was forced to sit in the first time I got looped back in time. It gave me the creeps just looking at it.

As I started to turn left out of the driveway, a few more trucks were pulling in. County Road

125 had gotten busier in the last hour. The steady traffic coming from the left hand side of the two lane road was beginning to annoy me. No let up. No way to make my turn. I was just about to give up and turn right in order to make a U-turn back when someone actually slowed down and let me go left. "I owe you, Buddy," I thought as I pulled into traffic but they were long gone.

Behind me, more cars and trucks pulled into the lumberyard. No wonder they were worried about a new road. But worried enough to commit a murder? I shrugged my shoulders and kept driving.

Chapter Seventeen:
Ajay

I was sure I was holding on to Aeden's wrist, but it felt different. As if the skin and flesh had disappeared altogether and the only thing left was bone. Something stinging and wet kept hitting my eyes and I just couldn't focus. Still, I was holding on to something. I just didn't know what. And for some reason, it took all of my energy just to spit out a few words.

"Aeden, are you there?"

"Stay where you are, Ajay!"

No matter how hard I tried, I just couldn't open my eyes and whatever was hitting my face and body stung me like a million icy scorpions. But the strange thing was how quiet everything had gotten. So quiet that it absolutely hurt my eardrums. A painful hurt. Still, I held on to the bone-like thing that was once Aeden's wrist. But I had no sense of my own body. Was I standing? Lying down? I had no idea. I only knew that I was trapped in something filmy – a combination of air, clouds and electricity. Again, I tried to scream for Aeden.

"Can you hear me?"

"Don't move, Ajay. It will pass."

What is she talking about? What will pass? What does she know? The sharp, cold needles that were hitting my face seemed to intensify. And then, I felt something grabbing my hand and pressing it tighter to the bone that I was holding. I wanted so desperately to pull away but I had no strength. Not even the slightest bit of energy. It was as if I had become nothing but air and electricity, no form or substance. I kept telling myself not to panic, but I felt as if I was about to lose control of the only thing I had left – my mind.

Then, in a flash, lights started to flicker and I took a fast fall to the ground, landing on top of a soft heap.

"Get off me, Ajay, it's over. Whatever it was, it's over."

The lights in the corridor were flickering and I could hear someone yelling from the stage.

"Where the hell is Phil? We're having a major problem with the lights!"

"A major problem with the lights?" I managed to stammer. "What the hell just happened?"

Aeden stood up quickly and looked around.

"A quick ripple in time, Ajay. Take a look at what's in your hand."

I never let go of Aeden's wrist. I swear it. But my fingers were wrapped around a solid chunk of bone.

As it fell to the ground my screams echoed through the hallway. I watched as Aeden bent down to pick it up.

"It's a tusk. Some sort of animal tusk."

Before I could say anything, a few of the theater kids came running down the corridor. All of them speaking at once.

"Have you seen Phil? The lights are a mess."

"What about Bobby and Ray? They know how to fix that stuff. Have you seen them?"

"Wow, where did you find that tusk? Better put it back in the prop closet. God knows how this stuff gets lost."

Aeden and I just stood there in the flickering light. But before we could answer, one of the girls gave us the strangest look and shook her head.

"What on earth were you two doing? You're both soaking wet!"

It took me a few seconds to grasp what had happened. And then it all made sense. The sharp stinging pangs I felt had to be ice particles hitting my face. Ice particles from some other time. Now, looped forward to a Missouri summer in 1952, they melted and soaked our clothing. Made my hair a mess, too. *Damn it!*

Aeden knows something. She's too laid back about this. She should be getting just as freaked out as I am but she's not. I looked down at my shirt and shuddered.

"Yeah, we were kind of fooling around at the sink and things got out of hand."

The girls in the corridor just laughed.

"Working Summer Theater will do that to you! Anyway, see if you can find Bobby or Ray. We've got to get the lighting fixed."

"Sure thing," Aeden said as the girls walked past us. Then she gave me a funny look.

"Do you know who they are?"

"Those girls or Bobby and Ray?"

"Any of them. There's like a zillion people working here."

"Yeah. So how come we were the only ones to get flipped back in time?"

"Because we're the only ones who don't belong here. Time is like an oyster, trying to get rid of anything foreign. Only instead of covering us in some gooey substance, it keeps spitting us up, all over the place until we eventually get back to where we belong."

"That's gruesome, Aeden. And creepy. I'm freaked out enough. My hair's a mess. I don't have make-up, God knows what condition my skin is in, and everything we eat is loaded with sugar and fat. And don't get me started about my lips. The only thing I have to protect them is some chapstick that one of the girls gave me. Not even with an SPF! And no gloss. No sheen. Just chapstick. I hate 1952!"

"Well, get used to it, Ajay, because I don't think we'd survive another flip back to the Ice Age."

Chapter Eighteen:
Ryn

County Road 125 was a fairly straight road but there were some steep drop-offs along the way. And those potholes could loosen the rope enough to send the lumber all over the place. Like it or not, I would have to obey the speed limit. Besides, I really didn't need anyone to ask for my license. I reached over to turn on the radio but all I got was some country western station with a lot of static. I turned it off. And that's when I felt the first jolt from the rear.

Someone had bumped the truck. The pile of lumber made it impossible for me to see what was going on and the side view mirrors didn't help. I sped up just a bit hoping that whoever was behind me would be satisfied. They weren't.

The next jolt. This time harder. *What is that moron's problem? Just pass me, you idiot. That's what you do on a dotted yellow line.* But the jerk behind me did it a third time. *OK, I'll slow down and pull over a bit to the shoulder so you can pass. Go ahead, moron. Just pass me.* This time the guy knocked into my rear bumper so hard that I was afraid it would fall off. *What is your problem?*

I thought about pulling off the road altogether but if the guy behind me was really in some sort of road rage, who knew what he'd do to me. So, I just kept driving. Speeding up enough to gain some distance and probably a ticket. But it wasn't as if I had a whole lot of choices.

The dirt road to the theater was at least seven or eight miles ahead. I just kept my foot on the gas. It had been a few minutes since the guy behind me rear-ended the truck. I figured maybe he was done. But I should have known better from my experience with that crazy woman, Margaux, last year in Paris. Crazy people never give up. And crazy people behind the wheel are real lunatics.

In a flash, I caught something in my left side view mirror. It had to be the truck who kept hitting me. *Well, go ahead and pass me. That's what you want to do.* I could see the front end of a large, dark colored truck as the cab approached me. Instinctively, I swerved a bit to the right, but it wasn't enough. Whoever was driving the truck sideswiped me just enough to send me off the shoulder for an instant. It happened so fast that I hardly noticed the fact that I was back on the road with the truck behind me once again.

This is insane. Now it's getting personal. What does that jerk want?

There was no place to pull off and the dirt road to the Playhouse was still a good five or six miles ahead. I just had to keep going. I hoped that there would be enough cars in the other lane so that the nut job behind me couldn't sideswipe me again. I tried to lean out the window in order to get a better look but it was impossible. Whoever was driving that truck knew how to keep it directly behind me so that I couldn't get a good look.

Five or six miles doesn't sound like much, but when the guy behind you thinks this is the demolition derby, every mile feels like ten. I just held my breath and kept going. But my body was tensing up. I knew that they weren't done with me. *Try to relax. If he hits you and you're relaxed, you won't get hurt that much. You'll only get hurt if you tense up.* Yeah, tell that to the cognitive part of my brain.

This time I expected to see him in my side view mirror and I was right. He had caught a break from a slowdown in traffic in the opposite lane and came up on the side of my truck with a vengeance. I braced myself, started to edge to the shoulder but it was too late.

He slammed my truck with enough force to send me over the shoulder and down a steep grade into a field of rocks. *Hasn't this stupid state ever heard of guard rails?* I took my foot off the gas and let the truck roll to a stop as I looked back to see where the guy was but all I could see was the steady traffic on the road. Wherever he was, or whoever he was, I wasn't going to find out today. Then, I felt something really hard knock into the back of my foot. Something had rolled out from under the driver's seat. *Great. Now what?*

I bent down and reached behind my foot to grab whatever it was, figuring that someone from the Playhouse left some tools there just in case. *Probably a hammer. It was heavy enough.* But the minute my hand grasped the metal, I knew it wasn't a hammer. Unless hammers had butts and bullets. I was looking at a revolver and didn't need an explanation. This had to be the gun I thought Ajay had taken. But was it the gun that would eventually kill Hank Clayton?

Chapter Nineteen:
Aeden

"**C**ome on, Ajay, we'd better get back to work painting those Tudor walls," I said as we entered the barn section of the theater. "We'll let Ryn know what happened to us as soon as he shows up."

"OK, fine."

We didn't say another word and frankly, I was glad. I just didn't feel like talking to Ajay. I wanted so badly to trust her, but I knew I couldn't. She had to be lying about the gun. Why would a truck have bullets stashed in the glove compartment but not a gun? Ajay was smart enough. No matter what Ryn told her, she'd figure otherwise. She saw the .38 caliber bullets and didn't want to risk the chance that they might belong to the gun that killed her great-grandfather. So, if she got rid of the gun, he might be alive. Well, at least in her way of thinking about it.

Ajay followed me to the side table where the brushes and buckets were kept. Painting fake brown beams on large beige backgrounds was as boring as ever, but it gave us time to catch bits and pieces of the conversations going around all over us.

"I heard they're almost all sold out for opening night."

"No kidding."

"Hey, has anyone seen the large stapler?"

"Someone said that Councilman Barkley's going to be in the audience."

"That big dip-stick?"

"Yeah, the very one. But I'd rather see him than the dim-wit he's running against."

"I just hope whoever wins will use enough influence with the highway department so we won't have to close."

"It's all about payola. Greasy hands and all."

"I need the large stapler. Who's got it?"

"Hey, we need someone to help us with the lights. Is there anyone here who's not afraid of heights?"

A short, thin kid brushed against us as he headed to the stage. I whispered to Ajay.

"Whatever you do, don't volunteer us."

"What do you think? That I'm nuts? I'm not going to risk my life walking along some balance beam in the dark."

Just then, someone let out a huge scream and we all went running to the stage. I could hear some of the crew members yelling.

"It's blood! And some sort of dead animal!"

"Just hair, covered in blood! Sure it's not a prop?"

"For 'Brigadoon?' Are you nuts? There are no dead animals in 'Brigadoon.'"

"Then what is it?"

By the time Ajay and I reached the stairs that led to the front of the stage we could see that something was dangling from one of the light poles. Some of the girls were still screaming when Phil came running through the building.

"What the heck is going on? What's all the commotion? Did the damn stage collapse?"

The short, thin kid who had pushed past us, answered him.

"It's some sort of dead animal, or parts of a dead animal, hanging from one of the light poles."

"So get it down! It's probably a raccoon that got in here and got fried from the lights. No big deal."

"Then how do you explain the blood?" one of the girls asked.

"He probably just got caught on something. Just get the carcass down. We don't have all day."

Then, all at once, the girls turned away and headed back to the barn area. I moved in closer to get a better look at the animal.

"It's not a raccoon, Ajay. Take a good look at its fur. It looks like part of one of those wild boars with the tough hide."

"I know," she said as she held up her hands for me to see. "There wasn't enough light in the corridor to take a good look, but see for yourself, Aeden, my hands are covered in blood."

Then, as if on cue, she started to cry.

Chapter Twenty:
Ryn

“**I**'m telling you, Nick, someone deliberately tried to run me off the road. I'm lucky I'm still in one piece. *Yeah, I'm lucky I didn't go crashing through the windshield 'cause you guys haven't invented seatbelts yet!* And that's not all."

Nick was eyeballing the damage to the driver's side of the truck. He didn't say anything at first, but kept shaking his head.

"Well, at least you're all right. Did you get a good look at the other car? Or a license plate?"

"No, it happened too fast. I could only tell that it was a larger truck than this one and a dark color, like a dark brown. I'm really sorry, Nick."

"Nah, it's not your fault. Playhouse has insurance. I'm going to call the sheriff and our insurance company. Sure you're OK?"

"Yeah, I'm fine. And the truck is running good, too. I was able to drive it straight up that incline without a problem. I think the only damage is to the body. But there's one more thing."

I wasn't sure what to say or do about the gun.

If Nick hid it in the truck and it went missing, then he'd know I had it. Heck, anyone would know. I was the last one to get behind the wheel. I put it back under the seat once I got back on the road, too freaked out to do anything else. But now, I was face to face with the one guy who might have some answers. And I wasn't about to waste any time.

"There's a gun under the front seat of the truck. When I slid off the road, the gun slid forward and knocked right into the heel of my foot. Geez, Nick, I was driving a truck with a gun in it. Aren't there laws against that?"

I expected Nick to do one of two things – get really pissed or scared. Pissed off that someone discovered where he stashed the gun or scared that someone knew he had it. But he wasn't the least bit concerned. In fact, he started laughing.

"The gun's a prop, Ryan. Left over from some old western play we did years ago. We put it in the truck just in case someone got threatened. Figured it would scare off anyone who approached the driver. Frankly, I forgot all about it until just now. Didn't mean to scare the daylights out of you."

I've seen fake guns before. Mostly plastic. But this was 1952. Maybe they didn't have plastic guns. Maybe this really was a fake. A prop. Whatever. But it was heavy and I doubted they used heavy guns as props. Still, I wasn't about to argue with Nick. I could have told him about the bullets that Ajay found, but I had no reason to dig through the glove compartment and I sure as hell wasn't about to tell him that Ajay took the truck last night, or at least tried to. But something wasn't right. And when that's the case, everyone's a suspect, even if the murder didn't happen yet.

"Look Nick, before I start unloading the lumber, do me a favor and take another look at that gun."

Nick shrugged his shoulders and opened the driver's side door.

"I'm telling you, Ryan. It's a prop. But if it makes you feel better, here goes."

He reached under the seat and pulled out the gun, holding it face up in the palm of his hand.

"See for yourself. Fancy little western number with carved horses on the metal. Great little cap gun. Looks real, too."

I took a deep breath and looked at the gun. It was a prop all right, but it wasn't the gun that rolled out and hit my foot. Someone had switched it. And they did it between the time I got back to the Playhouse and the few minutes it took for Nick and me to walk back to the truck. *It couldn't have been Nick. He was in the barn part of the theater working on some scenery when I got there.*

"Yeah, I guess you're right. Must have been my imagination. Well, I'll just start un-loading the wood."

"Thanks, Ryan. You can drive the truck to the back of the theater by the barn side and add the lumber to the pile that's already there. I'll go see if I can find someone to help you."

Nick walked back to the building as I got behind the wheel again. I waited until he was a good distance from me and then leaned over to open the glove compartment. I reached my hand in slowly, expecting to grab a few bullets, but the only thing in the compartment was a pack of matches and the registration. Maybe whoever took the gun, took the rest of the bullets as well.

I glanced down at the paper and could see that the truck was registered to The Mark Twain Summer Playhouse. It was a company car. But who was the owner? And did they have a motive for murder?

*   *   *

I didn't like the idea of being separated from Aeden and Ajay. Not with that time ripple going on. But I had to fit in. Had to look like I belonged here. That meant doing what was asked of me by Nick and anyone else in charge. I was just relieved to see my sister and Ajay scarfing down some cold sandwiches with the rest of the crew as I approached the back of the kitchen. My fingers were sore from unloading the wood and I was starving.

"Hey, Ryan," Ajay shouted. "We saved you a tuna sandwich."

Soft white bread and mushy tuna with globs of mayonnaise. My mother would have snatched it out of my hand if she had seen it. But eating healthy was apparently not an issue in this decade.

Aeden gave me a cold stare as I sat down next to them. When she was sure no one else could hear us, she leaned over and spoke.

"Next time you go driving off somewhere could you please let me know ahead of time?"

"Do I need a permission slip?"

"For your information, Ajay and I got sucked back in time. Back to where we were. It was only a few seconds but it felt like forever. And it felt like we'd never get back."

"Crap! This whole time thing is so freaking unstable. Not like bef---."

"I heard that!" Ajay shouted. "Admit it! You were going to say the word *before*. I knew it! I knew it all along! This isn't the first time you and Aeden have done this. I'm not a dumb blond so don't try to deny it. I want to know the truth and I want to know it now!"

Chapter Twenty-one:
Aeden

I watched as Ryn gave me a quick nod and then I listened as he explained about great Auntie Zanne's prisms and the whole hoarder's nest we had to deal with. Then, I told Ajay about Paris and Uncle Henri's murder. All the while she kept tapping her foot and biting her lower lip. Finally, she spoke.

"So, you thought you'd do what? Go back and find out who killed my great- grandfather?"

"Yeah Ajay," Ryn said quietly. "But we didn't expect time to be so screwed up."

"*Screwed up* seems to be the right term for it," I added. "I mean, it's like the coils of a screw – the inside coil is the Ice Age and the outside coil is 1952. It's never worked like this before. That's what's so scary."

Ajay's eyes got wider.

"So we just keep going back and forth with no chance of getting back to our own century?"

Ryn reached across the table and grabbed her hand. I wasn't sure if he was trying to reassure her or just make sure she didn't start a scene.

"We'll get back to our own time. You've got to trust in the laws of physics and nature. I'm sure it's the energy from those solar flares that's messing with it. But we've got other problems right now. Someone tried to run me off the road. Not me, exactly, but whoever they believed was driving the Playhouse truck. And by the way, I saw the gun that held those bullets you found in the glove compartment. It was stashed under the seat. But someone switched it to a prop gun when I got back here."

I gave Ryn a quick look. *So Ajay didn't hide a gun after all. She was telling the truth all along.*

"So who do you think switched guns?" I said as I swallowed the last of the sugary artificial juice drink.

"Don't know, but there's lots of suspects. I got a ton of information at the local lumberyard and it seems as if everyone wants Hank Clayton to throw his weight on their side of this highway issue."

"So what did the car look like that tried to run you off the road?" I said.

"It wasn't a car. It was another truck. And a big one. The guy just kept coming at me and then pulling away. I swear, for a moment it looked as if there was a passenger in the seat but I can't be sure."

Ryn reached for another mushy tuna sandwich just as Nick came running toward us.

"Hey Ryan! Something you need to know. I

just got off the phone with the sheriff and it turns out they had a truck stolen from a dealership in Marshfield. It was dark brown like the one you described. Dealer called the color 'Oxford Maroon.' And that's not all. Shortly after the truck was stolen, someone roughed up a team of highway surveyors by highway 28 and kidnapped one of them. The sheriff's going to want to talk to you. Meet me in the ticket office at the front of the building. He's on his way."

"Sure thing," Ryn said as he bit into the sandwich and glanced at me. I knew him well enough to recognize that look. He was piecing all of the details of that incident together in his mind and trying to make sense of them. It was a calculated, methodic approach that seemed to work for him. Then, he stopped chewing for a split second and took a step closer to Ajay and me, looking over his shoulder to make sure Nick was out of range.

"My God, Aeden," he exclaimed. "The guy in the truck wasn't trying to run me off the road. He was trying to get my attention!"

"You mean...."

"Yeah, I think it was Hank Clayton and he was being held at gunpoint. Forced to be behind the wheel."

Ajay jumped in before I could say a word.

"You've got to help him, Ryn. That guy is going to kill him. You know that. You can't have that on your conscience. I don't give a hoot about the time-space thing. You need to do the right thing. And do it NOW!"

And as much as I felt like shaking Ajay by the shoulders, I agreed with her, even if my brother didn't.

"Maybe we were meant to change history, Ryn. We don't know. But I'll tell you one thing. If we just let Hank Clayton die, we'll have to live with that for the rest of our lives."

"OK, fine. I give up! There's only so much nagging and whining a guy can take without losing it! So, screw the time-space continuum. Is that what you want? I can't be responsible for everything! But if the 21st century gets all messed up, don't blame me!"

Dr. Wesley Jamison brushed the thin gray wisps of hair across his forehead as he took another look at the report that was sitting on his desk. Then, he stood up, walked across the lab to the coffee pot and poured himself another cup.

"Something's not right or someone's playing a hell of a joke on us."

He picked up the phone and made a quick call to his colleague, Professor Lydia Garrison.

"Lydia, do me a favor and humor me. I've just gotten a report back from three of our labs – Fast Neutron Activation Analysis, Thermal Instrumental Neutron Activation and your lab, Inductively Coupled Plasma Mass Spectrometry. All of them say the same thing. That fragments from lead alloy are imbedded in the partial skull of a saber-tooth tiger. Now either that creature was roaming around Missouri in the last century or someone had a damn gun in the Ice Age!"

"That would be one hell of an expensive joke for someone to pull and no credible scientist would waste time and resources. Where did you say this sample came from?"

"A fossil dig in western Missouri. One of my lab assistants has a friend in the department of geographical sciences at the University of Missouri and guess what? Their lab results were the same. They thought it was a malfunction with their mass spectrometer so they sent the sample here."

"I'll be right over. I just need to make a few quick calls."

"No rush. It's taken the labs three months to complete the analysis. A few more minutes isn't going to make a difference."

Dr. Jamison read the report again and shook his head. Then, he picked up the phone and dialed the university operator.

"This is Dr. Wesley Jamison in Elemental Analysis. I need to be connected with the director of high energy physics. It's of the utmost importance."

"One moment sir. I'll see that your call goes right through."

Dr. Jamison inhaled and held his breath until he could hear a voice at the other end of the line. Then, he paused for a moment and spoke.

"I've just received three verified neutron analyses and the results will concern you."

Chapter Twenty-two:
Hank Clayton

Hank Clayton opened the refrigerator and took a quick gulp of the orange juice that his wife had just squeezed a few minutes before.

"Sorry Margie, I've got to run. I need to check on the surveyors out by Route 28, and then meet with the mayor's committee in town. I've got to deliver that state report to them."

"Hank, you need to tell them about the threats you've been getting. I don't like this a bit."

"It's nothing, Margie. Just blowhards trying to scare me."

"Well, it's working, because I'm scared."

"Don't be. If someone really wanted to harm me, they wouldn't take the time to send me an anonymous letter. Postage costs money you know. All they want is for me to swing my vote in their favor over this highway deal."

"Isn't that extortion or something?"

"It's stupidity, that's what it is and I intend to ignore it."

"I'll be glad when the vote's over and we can get on with our lives."

"Me, too. I'll be back in time for dinner. Don't burn the Salisbury steak!"

Margie gave her husband a quick hug and turned toward the sink. She could hear the squeak of the screen door followed by Hank's footsteps as he raced to the car. Pausing for a minute, she listened for the familiar slam of the front driver's side door, unaware that it was the last time she'd hear that sound.

Hank Clayton followed a winding dirt road until it merged with one that had recently been oiled.

"Damn it!" he thought. "I must have told the highway department a million times to put up signs when they oil these roads. It's going to take me hours to clean off this mess on my car. At least the state road has pavement and that's just a few miles ahead."

In the distance, Hank could see the two surveyors in their orange bibs off to the side of the road, just above a small berm. The new Gurley Transit System, with its tripods and telescoping lenses, was carefully laid out in a distinct triangle.

As he pulled the car off the road and onto the edge of the berm, one of the men waved to him. Hank ambled up the small hill and gave them a shout.

"How's it going? You fellows getting used to the new equipment?"

"It's going smoothly, boss," one of them answered. "Nothing like having modern equipment from 1950. I guess the state had to spring for it with the new project and all."

Hank nodded. "It should move things along quicker and everyone seems to be in a spittin' hurry to get this project going."

Before he could say another word, the men heard a rustling sound coming from the woods behind them.

"Probably a doe," one of them said. "They've been all over the place today. Spooked or something."

Hank turned to look, but what stood just a few feet from him was no deer. It was the barrel of a gun pointed directly at his face.

"Don't any of you move," came the muffled voice of a man whose mouth was covered with a dark bandana. "Just stand right where you are and no one gets hurt."

The surveyors remained motionless as a second figure emerged from the woods, also wearing a bandana over his mouth and pointing a gun.

"We're not carrying money with us," one of the surveyors started to explain.

"Shut up! All of you get on the ground, face down. NOW! QUICKLY!"

"Don't try anything," Hank said as he started to drop to his knees. "We'd better do as they say."

"Look out, boss," one of the surveyors shouted, but it was too late. The heavier of the two men clipped the side of Hank's head with the base of the gun. Stumbling forward, Hank Clayton tried to right himself but couldn't. He stumbled to his knees and remained there, steadying himself with one hand on the ground.

"Grab his keys," the man said as he turned toward his partner. "When we're done tying these guys up, you can ditch his car somewhere deep in the woods. So deep they won't find it until it's rusted over."

The lanky guy took a step back and seemed to swallow his own breath before speaking.

"Um, uh...there's only enough rope to tie up two of them. I meant to get more, but..."

"You moron! You brainless twerp! How am I going to explain that we forgot the rope? Never mind. Just tie up the two guys over there. Face down. And not just their hands. Tie up their feet and run the rope through their mouths. Don't need any canaries chirping in the woods."

"Sure thing. Sure thing," the man replied. "This'll work, boss. Won't it?"

"Idiot! It would have been easier just to toss ole Mr. Clayton here in the bed of the truck and cover him up with a tarp, but now, seeing as we don't have enough rope, I'll need to keep the gun pointed at him and that means he's got to do the driving."

"What about me?" the man said as he untangled a small coil of rope that dangled from his back pocket.

"What about you? You've got to take care of Clayton's car. Then hitch a ride back to town."

"How am I going to explain why I need a ride?"

"Think of something. And if you can't, then just walk!"

The man knew enough not to push his partner any further. He'd seen what happened to others who didn't know how volatile Darnell Legrun was. So, moving quickly, he snatched the car keys from Hank Clayton's jacket and immediately got to work tying up the surveyors.

Although his head was pounding from the blow, Hank managed to stand up and speak.

"I don't know what you're after, but you're going to get caught. Missouri has tough laws for assault."

"Keep talking buddy boy and you'll wish it was just assault."

Then, he pointed the .38 caliber pistol directly at Hank's face and motioned for him to walk through the edge of the woods.

"Got a pretty little brown truck waiting down the road a bit and you're going to be behind the wheel. No funny stuff. Just do as I say and maybe this will turn out to be an assault after all."

"Just leave the surveyors alone," Hank replied. "I imagine it was me you were after all along."

"You're worth a lot of money to me, Mr. Clayton. And the funny thing is, it doesn't matter if you're dead or alive. Just out of the way. So if I were you, I'd try real nice to keep my mouth shut and don't pull any crap when you get behind the wheel. Now, get going! We don't have all day!"

As Hank walked slowly to the thick line of trees, Darnell gave his partner a final shout.

"Stop diddling around and get going! You've already screwed up the plans. Just hope it ain't going to cost us!"

The man didn't reply. He knew better. He also knew that this boss liked keeping things simple. And a dead body would be a hell of a lot less complicated than dealing with a live one.

And Hank had just figured that out, too.

Chapter Twenty-three:
Ryn

If it wasn't bad enough that the harpy tag team of Aeden and Ajay had succeeded in getting me to re-think things, Aeden goes and springs something else on me.

"I am going to be in this play, Ryn! One of the girls sprained her ankle and can barely walk. Marcy asked me to step in. What could I say?"

"No. You could say no!"

"I can't afford to let my talent go to waste. You've heard me. I can sing. And you've seen me. I can dance. "

"She's right, you know," Ajay chimed in. "Aeden was always so talented when it came to the stage."

"That was in freaking fifth grade, Ajay!" I yelled, loud enough that I swore the veins in my head were going to burst. "This isn't elementary school. Hell, this isn't even school! And if my sister wants to go on the misguided perception that she's the next Ann Hathaway or Zooey Deschanel, then good for her! Yeah, don't look so shocked. You two aren't the only people who've seen movies lately. And I'm telling you, this is a bad idea."

"You're jealous of my talents, Ryn," Aeden replied, lifting her nose slightly into the air.

"The two of you are insane. But let me get this straight. You want me to find out who kidnapped Ajay's great-grandfather while you both go singing and dancing your way through some lousy summer theater show?"

Ajay took a step toward me and touched my elbow.

"Not exactly. Aeden will be on stage for 'Brigadoon,' but you and I can work together tracking down Hank Clayton's kidnappers."

"Terrific," I muttered. "All we need to do is find Scooby-Doo and we've got it made."

"That's what I like about you, Ryn. You've got such a neat sense of humor."

I wanted to vomit. Or at least gag but I didn't. Aeden wasn't the only one in the family with acting talents. I glanced out the small window in the kitchen and could see the sheriff's car pulling up.

"I told Nick I'd meet him at the ticket office. Alone. I'll catch up with you later."

"You'd better not keep anything from us," Aeden said as I left the room.

"Wouldn't dream of it."

I could feel the burning stares on my neck as I exited the room. My sister had become insufferable. And Ajay...well, I really was at a loss for words.

The tuna sandwich seemed to jell in my mouth as I rounded the outside of the building. In seconds, the bread, mayonnaise and canned fish had formed a sticky lump in my throat. I swallowed hard and stepped into the tiny room, catching Nick by surprise. He turned around from the desk and started to speak. I could tell by the tight expression on his face that something else was on his mind. Something that didn't involve a kidnapping.

"Hey, Ryan. Thanks for hurrying over. Looks like kidnapping won't be the only thing the sheriff will have to be dealing with."

"What do you mean?"

"Someone broke into the small safe in this office and stole a boatload of money."

"Are you sure it was broken into and not someone who made a deposit or something?"

"Yeah, I'm sure. I'm the only one who makes the deposits. And this was no small chump change. We're talking five grand."

"Five thousand dollars?" My voice seemed to jump an octave. *That would be at least 25 thousand today.* "Who keeps that kind of money in a small safe?"

"It was from a wealthy theater donor. To help with expenses, like a new roof. I meant to go to the bank yesterday. Hell, I didn't want all that cash sitting around. But things got kind of hectic around here so I put it off until today. Then, when I went to the safe, I saw it was broken into. Someone cracked open the lock with a crowbar or something. See for yourself."

The safe looked like one of those metal green school lockers you see in the old movies, only it had two doors, two handles and a combination lock. Both handles were smashed apart as well as the lock. Someone went to a lot of trouble to pry the doors open. Someone who wasn't afraid of making noise.

"Who else knew about the money?"

"Heck, everyone. We wanted to share the good news with the cast and crew. You must have been on your way to the lumberyard when it was announced."

I don't know why, but I had a nagging suspicion that these two events were somehow related.

"Do you think whoever stole the money had something to do with the kidnapping?"

Nick shook his head.

"Usually people get kidnapped because someone wants ransom money. Not the other way around."

I wasn't convinced.

"What if someone stole that money so they could use it in order to pay someone else to do the kidnapping?"

"Sounds kind of farfetched if you ask me. Anyway, that's why we have a sheriff. Let him investigate. Meanwhile, it looks as if I'll be bothering the insurance company again. And I hate to think what that's going to do to our rates."

"I'm sorry, Nick. Really. I can't help but feel as if the truck thing was my fault. Maybe I should have just pulled off the road."

"No. You did the right thing. Just tell the sheriff everything you remember. Ralph Hutchins isn't your typical country bumpkin sheriff. He may not be college educated, but he's a decent investigator. Got a good reputation around here and that's not easy."

The lump from the tuna sandwich was still lodged somewhere in my throat and I swallowed again. How could I tell the sheriff that I thought Hank Clayton was the guy who was kidnapped? What possible reason could I give? Then, something flashed across my mind and I started to relax. After all, they found the surveyors. That meant they already knew Hank Clayton was taken. But what none of us knew was whether or not he was still alive.

Chapter Twenty-four:
Darnell Legrun

Darnell looked over his shoulder, satisfied that his partner managed to tie up the two surveyors. It was bad enough that the guy was such a bumbling idiot, but worse yet, he was Darnell's brother-in-law. And whatever possessed his sister to marry Randy Tinger was something Darnell would never understand. Then, he gave Hank a slight nudge with the tip of the gun as they made their way through the thick line of trees.

"Just keep walking. And keep your mouth shut."

The plan had fizzled right under Darnell's nose the minute he found out that Randy hadn't bothered to get enough rope. Hank Clayton was not supposed to recognize either of the men. But now, it was evident that Darnell would have to take his bandana off once they got into the truck. He couldn't risk anyone seeing him in the front seat wearing something over his mouth. It was a dead giveaway. And with that, Darnell knew he needed another plan.

"Stupid Randy," he thought to himself. "We were just supposed to snatch this Hank guy and keep him locked up for two days. Three at max. Then, all we had to do was dump him in some back little town and collect our money. Such an easy way to make a few grand. But now, hell, now I've got to figure out something else."

Darnell's tongue moved over to the spot in the back of his mouth where a tooth was missing. He liked the feel of the hard gum between his teeth, like a little cave folded into the mountains. And that's when it occurred to him. Caves! This place was thick with caves. Heck, even Jesse James had a hideout in one of them. He'd stash Hank Clayton deep in a cave. But he'd have to do something to make sure the guy couldn't get out. And with no rope or anything to tie him up, that wasn't going to be so easy.

For a brief second, Darnell thought about shooting him in the leg, just to slow him down. But what if he bled to death? They weren't supposed to kill Hank Clayton, only make him disappear for a while. Darnell's hand trembled slightly as he motioned Hank forward, knowing that if he didn't come up with a better solution, then he'd have no choice but to make sure a bullet got lodged somewhere between Hank's knee and foot.

Hank could see the brown truck through the branches. They were nearing the road. His head ached but at least the dizziness had stopped.

"Get in the passenger's side and slide over to the driver's side," Darnell ordered. "And don't pull any funny stuff. I'm going to be sitting right next to you with a gun aimed at your stomach."

Hank slid into the seat and glanced at the dashboard. It was a Chevy. Only a year or two old. He doubted it belonged to the guy with the gun.

"Take the keys and start driving. Slowly. All the way up to the 125."

As Hank pulled onto the road, Darnell yanked the bandana off and let it drop to the floor.

"Just keep your eyes on the road and do as I say."

Traffic was usually sparse on Route 28 and today was no different. Hank did as he was told until they reached State Route 125. Then, he seized the only opportunity he had to get someone's attention.

The Mark Twain Playhouse Truck had just cleared the lumberyard when Hank spied it in the distance. Wasting no time, he edged the Chevy forward and bumped the rear of the smaller truck, enough to jostle the plywood and beams that were piled up in the truck's bed.

"What are you trying to do?" Darnell yelled. "I told you to go slowly."

But Hank refused to listen. He knew that Darnell wasn't about to fire off his gun and get them both killed. So he jolted the theater truck again. This time a bit harder, hoping that the driver would take notice.

Then, he felt a sudden jab in his stomach as Darnell pushed the barrel of the gun into it.

"I mean it. Slow down if you know what's good for you. I have no problem pulling the--"

Darnell never got to finish his sentence. Hank gave the theater truck one final bump before pulling out and sideswiping it, only to tail it tightly from behind, hoping that whoever was at the wheel would get a good look at him.

"Enough of your crap," Darnell yelled, shoving the barrel of the gun so deep into the driver's stomach that Hank gasped for air. And that's when he hit the gas, swerved to the right and ran the little theater truck straight off the road.

"Whoever you are behind that wheel, take a good look at me," Hank muttered under his breath. "It may be the last look anyone gets."

Chapter Twenty-five:
Aeden

"I think Ryn would rather work alone on this," I said as Ajay watched him leave the kitchen. Everyone else was finishing up and getting back to the stage or the painting and prop area directly behind it. She was about to say something when Marcy rushed over to us.

"Eden, I can't tell you how thrilled we are that you agreed to step in for Betty Jean. It's a major role. You'll need to learn those lines and the dance routine by the weekend. Think you can manage it? I can work with you on the choreography."

I was ecstatic. This was the opportunity I needed to make a name for myself, even if that name was half a century before I was born. I couldn't push the words out of my mouth fast enough.

"Yes, yeah, of course, sure...I know that song. I know all of the songs from the show. I've been singing them for at least six or seven years."

Marcy laughed and shook her head.

"Boy, talk about being excited for a part. That show opened in 1947 on Broadway. Only five years ago, but that's fine, Eden. I know you'll do a great job. See you on stage in a minute."

"Hey, Marcy!" someone yelled. "You need to get over to Nick in the ticket office. The sheriff is there. Clarisse can get everyone started with the rehearsal."

Marcy's face froze for an instant, as if she were collecting her thoughts. Then, she took a quick breath and spoke to the messenger.

"Oh, it must be about the truck incident. I wonder why they would want to talk to me. Never mind. Tell Clarisse to begin with the opening number and use the understudy for my role. I'll be back in a jiffy."

Without bothering to say another word to me, Marcy darted out the door. But I wasn't the only one who caught that look on her face. Ajay had seen it, too.

"Did you see her face, Aeden? I swear that girl is hiding something."

"I have to admit, she looked kind of spooked, but maybe it's because the show opens in a few days and she didn't want to miss the rehearsal."

"Look, Aeden. I know you have to be on stage. But I don't and they won't miss me. I'm going to sneak over to the rear of the ticket office. The back of the prop area shares the same wall. I'll try to listen in on any conversation. If anyone walks in on me, I'll just pretend I was looking for something."

As much as I didn't want to admit it, Ajay had a good idea. We needed as much information as possible and as far as I was concerned, anyone could have had something to do with the kidnapping.

"OK, Ajay. If anyone asks for you, I'll tell them you're sorting props."

"No matter what he says, Ryn needs my help. Even Sherlock Holmes needed that other guy."

"Watson?"

"What son? Whose?"

"Never mind, just go. They're already calling for the cast to be on stage. I've got to run."

Ajay headed straight for the prop area as if she had done this a million times. I took my spot backstage waiting for the first chorus number. Within seconds, we were dancing, stomping, twirling and singing. Nothing had ever felt as glorious. I belonged here. I knew it. Maybe time brought us back for a reason.

And then, in an instant, the music stopped. The house lights came on and the next voice I heard wasn't an actor.

"Sorry to interrupt your rehearsal, but it seems as if we've got a bit of a problem. I'm going to need everyone to take a seat in the audience and remain there. I need to ask each and every one of you some questions."

"Is this some sort of joke?" I whispered to the girl standing next to me.

"Sheriff Hutchins isn't the type to joke around."

I took a good look at the robust guy who was making his way down the aisle. Ryn and Nick were walking quickly behind him, but Marcy was nowhere to be seen.

Chapter Twenty-six:
Darnell Legrun

Darnell watched as the Mark Twain Playhouse truck careened off the road. Then he pulled the gun away from Hank's stomach and spoke.

"Don't know what crap you're trying to pull but it won't work. Keep driving and make the next turn-off."

Hank did as he was told. He could hear the crunch of the hard packed gravel as they turned onto number 88 Road. He knew the spot and his chest tightened. Number 88 Road led to a series of small caves. Few houses on this road and one or two pastures that belonged to local farmers. The chances of being spotted were slim.

"Just do as I say and the gun won't go off," Darnell said after motioning Hank to park the truck near the entrance to one of the caves. He slid out, still keeping the barrel pointed at the driver's side.

"Now move it," Darnell continued. "Get out and walk directly into the cave."

If he remembered correctly, there was a small drop-off in one of these caverns. Darnell had played there as a kid. But which cave? They hadn't all day and his options were limited. Still, it was better than nothing. *If only that pea-brained brother-in-law of mine had remembered the rope.* But it was too late to do anything about it. Darnell was stuck and when people get stuck, they act like animals in a trap. Darnell was no different. Fighting back a growing panic, he motioned Hank forward.

Taking the worn leather embossed cigarette lighter from his pocket, Darnell flicked it open as they stepped inside the cave. For a brief second, he stifled a laugh. *I was gonna break this cigarette habit years ago. Good thing I didn't bother.*

Hank took slow, deliberate steps in the darkness. The slight flame coming from the lighter was hardly enough to illuminate the space. Still, it was better than nothing, but Darnell was getting impatient.

"Quit stalling and walk," he grumbled as Hank tried to make his way in the semi-darkness. "I don't have all day and I need to find a nice, cozy little drop-off for you."

Time seemed to be at a standstill for Darnell as the men moved deeper into the cave. "Maybe it was another one of these caverns," he thought, "that had the drop-offs." Then his thoughts turned as dark as the cave itself.

I can't take the risk and have this Hank guy identify me. Damn that stupid Randy. This was such a simple deal. Now his idiocy is going to convolute everything. Even if I had rope and tied the guy up, someone might come across him. Kids play in and out of this place all the time. A regular underground Romper Room. No, there's only one thing I can do and I should have done it sooner.

Darnell moved closer to Hank and raised his arm, pointing the barrel of the gun directly at the back of the man's head. He could feel a slight waver in his wrist, forcing him to grip the gun even tighter. His finger circled the trigger guard. Then, without hesitation, he pulled the trigger back, firing a clear, straight shot.

The noise was deafening, reverberating around the walls of the cave and bouncing into crevices and chasms. The pain in his head made him wish he hadn't taken that shot. Not here. Not in the cave. But it was too late. Because in that instant, that brief second when the bullet pierced through space, time had folded, taking both men into its crease.

PART TWO:
TIME TWISTS

Chapter Twenty-seven:
Ajay

I nearly dropped the glass that I had pressed against the wall when I heard someone yelling for the entire cast and crew to report to the stage. What the heck! I didn't even get a chance to hear anything in the ticket office. What a colossal waste of time. I thought that sheriff would never finish with his questions.

"Where were you? What were you doing? Do you have any reason to...?" Good grief – this was worse than my mother's interrogations if I broke a stupid curfew or something. I could tell Aeden wasn't too pleased, either, but all she kept doing as we sat in our seats waiting for the sheriff to finish was take deep breaths and talk about stage names.

"I have it narrowed down to three names, Ajay. Barbara Eden, Eden Moon, or Eden Eve."

"I think someone already has the first name and the others sound like bath soaps or shower gels."

"Now you're sounding just like Ryn. Honestly, Ajay."

I was about to respond when all of a sudden, the room got really cold. At first I thought maybe someone had turned on an air-conditioning unit but then I remembered where we were and the fact that the Playhouse didn't have air-conditioning. It had overhead fans and none of them were moving.

Aeden nudged my arm, but as I turned to face her, everything had gotten darker and the cast and crew were starting to freak.

"Quit screaming! It's probably just a storm."

"It's pitch black in here. What happened to the lights?"

"I'm freezing. Worse than winter. What's going on?"

"Can anyone see anything?"

Then I recognized the sheriff's voice above the crowd.

"Stay in your seats. It'll pass. Just a weird storm."

Then a high pitched panicked voice followed.

"A tornado. I bet it's a tornado."

"There's no wind!" the sheriff yelled. "It's probably an eclipse."

"I know it's 1952," I whispered to Aeden, "but didn't they have prior warnings about those things?"

"Shh, the guy just doesn't want anyone to panic. Stop talking for a second and take a deep breath. Do you smell it?"

I thought I'd gag. It was primal. Intense and irritating. Like the smell you'd expect in a butcher shop or slaughterhouse. And I knew in that moment the Playhouse was gone and we were back in time. But not just Aeden, Ryn and me. Everyone. Their shrieks, at first intense and loud, became muffled and garbled. I could still hear them but it was as if they were yelling from across a chasm or something.

"My God," Aeden yelled, "Not again."

By now Ryn had made his way over to us.

"Just ride it out. We'll be fine."

"Shut up, Ryn," I yelled back. Was he nuts? *Ride it out.* You don't *ride out* things like this. The muffled voices in the background became garbled as if people were talking underwater, or at least trying to. I kept waiting for my eyes to adjust to the darkness but they didn't. At least not right away. I grabbed the bottom of my chair to convince myself that some things were still real. There was a word for that but my mind was foggy and by the time I realized what it was, the chair was gone and I had to catch myself from falling. Then I remembered. *Tangible.* The word was tangible.

By now my body was shivering uncontrollably. I tried rubbing my arms and shaking my feet. Anything to stop the cold. Was it night back in the Ice Age? Is that why I couldn't see anything? But there had to be stars. The stars were older than earth itself. I tried focusing straight ahead and that's when the blast pierced my ears. A bomb. Had someone set off an atomic bomb? It was 1952. OH MY GOD! OH MY GOD! NUCLEAR TESTING! That's what they did back then.

I was just about to scream when I saw a quick burst of light coming from the distance, long enough for me to see a tall man pointing a gun. But there was nothing in front of him. Then, the darkness started to fade and we were back in the Mark Twain Playhouse.

The lights came on and everything looked normal again, except for the fact that the cast and crew were flipping out.

"What happened?"

"Must have been a weird electrical storm."

Then I heard Phil's voice.

"Call off rehearsal until we can check every wire, plug and outlet! Crew members – get to center stage NOW!"

But the sheriff had other ideas.

"Everyone stay seated until we finish up. If you've already been questioned and you're needed on the stage, then go. Otherwise, stay in your seats."

I turned to Ryn and Aeden to tell them what I saw but as things turned out, they already knew.

Chapter Twenty-eight: Ryn

"**A**re you sure you don't remember anything else? You know, kid, even the smallest detail, something you think's insignificant, can turn out to be a real clue."

I stared at the sheriff and tried to stop myself from bursting out laughing. I wanted to tell him that that line would become the standard for every cop show in the next five decades. But all I did was shake my head.

"Sorry. Other than the fact that the truck was brown, and bigger than the one from the Playhouse, that's all I can tell you. Like I said before, 'whoever was driving it bumped into me and then ran me off the road.' At first I thought it was personal. Not me, but maybe they thought someone else was driving the Playhouse truck. But if you really want my opinion, I think it was Hank Clayton behind the wheel."

"WHAT?"

"The way the guy drove...it was as if he was trying to get my attention. To warn me. But I didn't catch on. When I turned off the state highway, the brown truck didn't follow me. If someone had it 'in' for me, they would have been right behind me."

"Kid's got a point," the sheriff said as he glanced at Nick. "I'm going to notify the other jurisdictions on the state highway and see if they know anything. Meanwhile, I'll have some of my men check out the smaller roads just off the 125. Now what's this about a theft? You want to make sure I earn my keep?"

Nick explained about the money and the broken safe as the sheriff took notes.

"I can have my deputy dust the thing for fingerprints but unless the robber is someone who was arrested in this state, I doubt it will help. And, it will take weeks for the results. Still, I suppose it's a start. But questioning people and listening out for rumors is still the best way to solve these things. Might as well start now with your cast and crew. You say they all knew about the money?"

"Yeah," Nick replied. "We, I mean Marcy and I, were so excited about the donation that we just wanted to share the good news."

The sheriff flipped the paper over on his small pad.

"Who's this Marcy?"

"She's the stage manager and an actress. Been with the Playhouse for a few years."

"Well, I'd like to speak with this Marcy first."

Nick waved his arm and replied.

"They're probably rehearsing right now."

The sheriff closed his note pad and walked to the door.

"Looks like that rehearsal's going to have to wait a bit. Come on, let's get moving."

I followed Sheriff Hutchins and Nick into the theater, looking over my shoulder hoping to spot Aeden or Ajay. But before I could make my way over to them, a tall girl with long blond hair raced over to Nick.

"Is Marcy with you? We really need help with this number."

"With me? I thought she was in the stage area."

"No, she left a while ago. Got a message that you wanted to see her in the office."

"I did," Nick replied. "But she never showed up. I thought she got tied up."

Then, Nick grabbed me by the shoulder as the sheriff continued walking to the stage.

"Ryan, you've already talked to the sheriff and I'm needed here to help out with this mess, so… you mind running over to the girls' cabin to see if Marcy is there?"

"Sure." I was about to say "no problem" when I realized that expression wasn't around in 1952. Luckily, I caught myself.

"I'll be right back."

Nick mumbled something as he rushed down the aisle to catch up with the sheriff. I turned the other way and went out the main door and headed to the girls' cabin.

No sign of Marcy anywhere and I wasn't about to check out the outhouse. I have my limits where favors are concerned. Glancing at the driveway, I could see that the theater truck was still there. She had to be somewhere around here but I wasn't about to play hide and seek. I just wanted to get back to the theater. For some odd reason, I felt as if something wasn't right. And it had nothing to do with kidnappings or thefts.

Holy crap. I'm becoming worse than Aeden. Imagining all sorts of weird stuff. But it seems to be getting darker and I'm sure as hell not imaging that!

My feet felt like dead weight but I forced myself to keep moving until I reached the double wooden doors that opened into the Playhouse. By now, everything was dark and all I could hear was screaming. Outside, the air was calm. Almost deadly still. And in that second, I knew just what had happened.

Chapter Twenty-nine:
Marcy Meadows

Marcy left the kitchen and turned in the direction of the ticket office as soon as she got the word that Nick needed to see her. But instead of rounding the building, she darted into the wooded area where the cabins were located and grabbed the old blue Schwinn bike that once belonged to a former cook. Wasting no time, she checked her small purse to make sure there were coins in it, and then, peddling as fast as she could down the driveway, headed to the only gas station-repair shop between the Playhouse and the state highway.

The phone booth was located off to the side of the garage next to the small restrooms. A large sign that read "Get key from office" dangled between the restroom doors. Marcy rested the bike against the frame of the phone booth and stepped inside. Picking up the large black receiver, she deposited a dime and waited for the dial tone. Within seconds, a familiar voice was at the other end.

"Marcy! Is everything all right? I told you not to call this number unless it was an emergency."

"I thought you should know that the sheriff just showed up and is in Nick's office right now.

Probably about the theater truck, but I really needed to ask you something and it couldn't wait."

"Where are you calling from?"

"The service garage just off the highway. I biked here."

"You shouldn't have done that. They'll be looking for you. What did you want?"

"I know you said you didn't want to get involved again, but---"

"Look, Marcy. I've told you before. I'm done with that stuff. What you do is your business. I thought I made that clear."

"You did, but I think things are going to fall apart if you don't step in."

"I'm sorry, Marcy. But I can't."

"You mean you won't."

"You'd better hurry if you want to get back to the Playhouse before too long. Bye."

Before Marcy could say another word, the person at the other end of the receiver had hung up. Marcy could feel the heat burning in her cheeks but she bit her lip and slowly looked around. The two gas pumps were still vacant. No one had pulled in while she was on the phone. Relieved to have gone unnoticed, she threw her leg over the bar in front of the seat, and leaning forward to get more momentum, started peddling while standing.

It wasn't until she was a few yards down the road that she allowed herself to sit down and peddle comfortably. By the time she reached the Playhouse, the sheriff was just concluding his questioning.

"Marcy, where have you been? We've been looking all over for you!" Nick yelled as she made her way to the stage.

"I'm sorry. I was about to go to your office when I suddenly had a terrible stomach ache and had to go back to my cabin."

"I sent that Ryan kid over there. Didn't you hear him?"

"My stomach was really bad, Nick. I was running back and forth from the outhouse."

"Oh" was Nick's only reply before Marcy continued to speak.

"I'm feeling better now. It was probably that tuna fish. Anyway, what's going on?"

Nick quickly raced through the recent jumble of events as Marcy listened intently before saying a word.

"Our money is gone? Gone? Like that? Does the sheriff have any idea who took it?"

"That's why he's questioning everyone. And he'll want to talk to you as well."

"I have no idea who could have stolen the money. I thought the sheriff had come here to find out about the truck."

"Yeah, that, too."

"Well, I'd better get to the stage. The sooner we get this over with, the sooner we can get on with rehearsal."

"Wait a minute," Nick said as she started for the stage. "While you were going back and forth from the cabin to the outhouse, did you notice anything odd?"

"Like what?"

"Like a storm without the rain or wind."

"Huh?"

"I know that sounds pretty jerky, but everything in here went haywire, like I mentioned before. I thought maybe it was some sort of electrical storm."

"The only thing I noticed was the smell in the air. Like something putrid. I figured they were burning garbage in the old dump."

"Unless they've got a new method for waste disposal, I don't think it has anything to do with garbage. I just hope it doesn't happen again. We open in a few nights and we need good ticket sales to start the season."

"If they go through with this highway deal, Nick, it will be our last season. And I'll do anything to make sure that doesn't happen."

Nick could see Marcy's slender silhouette as she reached the stage. He knew that she was counting on the summer theater agents from the big cities to catch her performance. But how far would she really go to keep the Playhouse afloat?

"It's one thing to be determined," he thought. "But it's another to be desperate."

Chapter Thirty:
Ryn

I figured Aeden should've been used to this stuff by now, but I was wrong. And Ajay was making things worse. Why is it that when two girls get together their hysteria level multiplies exponentially? All I said was *ride it out* and you'd think I asked them to go careening off a cliff or something.

"Shh, Ajay. Keep it down. I know what you saw. I saw it, too."

Ajay leaned her face so close to mine that I could smell the mint gum she was chewing.

"Did you see the gun? That man, or the shape of a man, was pointing a gun."

"I didn't see a gun, Ajay. I saw two figures standing."

Then Aeden piped in.

"I saw someone pointing something and then the guy in front disappeared."

I tried to whisper as quietly as possible.

"This is so unreal. It's like all of us are seeing parts of the past at different time sequences."

Aeden wasted no time getting to the point.

"What the heck does that mean? Is time unraveling? Is that why events are being spit out in pieces? Oh my God, Ryn!"

"Look," I said, trying to keep my voice low, "I don't know. Probably not. But I'll tell you what I do know if both of you promise not to start screaming or freaking out. OK?"

"We won't freak, just tell us."

I took a quick breath before speaking. No one was near us but I wanted to hurry up, just in case.

"The time loop that's connecting 1952 to the Ice Age is tightening. It's taking less and less time for events in one era to suddenly flip into another."

Ajay all but swallowed her gum.

"You mean that we could be going back and forth every few minutes instead of every few days?"

"Yeah, that's it in a nutshell!" I said, clicking my tongue against the roof of my mouth as if I were describing how to operate a piece of machinery or something.

And even though my sister promised not to lose it, she did. Her voice got so loud that everyone turned to us.

"How can you be so flippant?"

Before I could utter a word, I heard Ralph Hutchins' voice yelling for everyone to stay seated, and for the first and probably only time in my life, I was relieved to be taking orders from the local law enforcement. It meant a quick reprieve from telling Aeden and Ajay the truth. The time loop was getting closer and closer until both eras collide. Was it because of those solar flares? Or maybe the electromagnetic pulse? I had no idea. I only knew that we needed to solve Hank Clayton's kidnapping and find a way back to our own time before things got even more screwed up. I just hoped my sister wouldn't be dancing her feet off on stage or worse yet, singing, when that moment came.

Chapter Thirty-one:
Aeden

I could tell Ryn was seething. He always grits his teeth and glares when he doesn't get his way. Well, I'm sorry. But for once in my life, I have an opportunity and I don't want to miss it. Besides, I thought Ajay was perfectly capable of helping my brother. How was I supposed to know that she would make things worse?

The rehearsal ended really late last night and I was exhausted. My eyes were burning the next morning as I hurried to the stage. Opening night was only three days away. The set was completely done and the crew was busy working on the Shakespeare one. And while they were doing that, Ryn was methodically asking people questions and trying to piece together any bits of information he could regarding the kidnapping.

We had a chance to speak briefly during a mid-morning break.

"They kidnapped the wrong person, Aeden. I swear. It should have been Ajay. She's driving me nuts. Every time I ask someone something, she just blurts out something else and gets them off track."

I shrugged and gave him one of my "can you ever forgive me" looks.

"Did you manage to find out anything at all?"

"Oh yeah. Lots of information. Say, did you know that Clarisse dyes her hair? Or that Nick turned down a teaching job at a community college near Rolla? Or maybe the fact that someone thought Councilman Barkley was having an affair! Yeah, I found out a hell of a lot of stuff! Trouble is, none of it has to do with the kidnapping!"

The ten minute break had ended and they were calling us back on stage when Ryn recognized someone walking past us.

"That's the guy who owns the lumberyard. Lon. Lon Percy. I wonder what he's doing here."

I turned and could see the guy motioning for Phil just as someone yelled, "Back to stage everyone!"

The two men slipped behind the curtain to the left and I could see a smile forming on my brother's mouth.

"I wonder why Lon Percy needs to talk to Phil."

"You can find out in a minute. They're going to shut the house lights and just have the stage lights on. No one will see you sneak behind the curtain."

"Terrific Aeden. Just terrific. I can go stumbling around in the dark trying to listen in on a conversation."

"Well, do you have a better idea?"

Ryn made some grumbling noise as he stepped toward the curtain, but before he slipped behind the heavy drapes, I just had to ask.

"What about Ajay? Where is she?"

"Shh...she's in the office working on the programs. She'll be out of my way for a while. If I find out anything I'll let you know."

I moved quickly to my spot on stage just as Clarisse shouted "Places everyone! Places!" Then the house lights dimmed and the pit band started the music. As I glanced at the curtain, I could see Ryn's back. Little did I know that the next time we would be together would be under very different circumstances.

Chapter Thirty-two:
Ryn

Eavesdropping is not my thing. It's creepy. Still, what choice did I have? Aeden couldn't do it and Ajay would only screw things up. Luckily, I could hear Phil and Lon without any trouble. They were speaking in low voices and I was just a few feet away. I could always claim that I was working props or something if I got caught.

I recognized Phil's voice first, because I heard it all the time as he ordered the light crew around.

"Wasn't there anything else we could have done?"

"Believe me, son, if there was, I wouldn't have resorted to this. But if we don't grease his greedy fat palms, then we can kiss our entire business good-bye. Years of establishing a name and reputation."

"Did you pay him all the money he asked for?"

"Yeah. And you know what that meant. But at least it will buy us some influence. Enough to prevent the highway from running through the lumberyard. And through the Playhouse for that matter. Think of all those jobs we just saved, including yours."

"But what if someone finds out what we did?"

"I doubt they will."

"Does mom know?"

"Of course not. And that doesn't sit well with me. I've never lied to your mother before. But I've never been in this position either. Anyway, I just stopped by to let you know that it's done. Money paid up and all."

"OK. I'll catch up with you in a few days. It's crazy around here. We open this coming weekend."

Just then, the music changed and a huge curtain sideswiped me. *Holy crap. It's the opening number and I'm too close to the stage.* I took a step forward and made a quick dive to the stage stairs, all but tumbling into the pit band.

"Watch it!" someone whispered. "No crew allowed in front once we start."

I had no intention of remaining in front of, or anywhere near, the stage. I had to find Nick and I needed to do so right away. By now, I was in the audience, congratulating myself for solving the theft. So...Phil was Lon's son and they stole the money to pay off some big shot who would make sure the highway vote goes their way. But what big shot? Hank Clayton? He didn't seem like the kind of guy who took bribes. The

Stocktons? They had more to gain by having the highway cut thought this little neck of the woods. That left Councilman Barkley or his opponent. Whoever that was. Or, for that matter, it could be anyone. I just didn't know who all the players were. And there wasn't enough time to find out.

By now my eyes had gotten accustomed to the darkness and I scanned the audience for Nick. Nothing. Clarisse seemed to be running the show. In all likelihood, Nick was in the office. *Oh no. In the office with Ajay. She's probably driving him insane with her stupid questions.* Without wasting a second, I bolted out of the rear exit and rushed to the office, ready to rat out Phil and Lon. But I never got the chance. Nick spoke before I could say anything.

"Ryan, I was just about to send Audrey Jane to look for you. The sheriff just called. They found the stolen truck. And you'll never guess where?"

"Um..er.."

"They found it in front of those caves, off of number 88 Road."

"Did they find anything else?"

"You mean, like a body or something? No. Just the stolen truck. Sheriff figures the kidnapper has Hank Clayton stashed somewhere in the caves. Left the truck there and had someone else pick him up."

"Did they find two sets of tires?" I demanded, sounding just like one of those TV detectives.

"I don't know what they found; but they didn't find Hank. That's why I was going to get you. The sheriff's starting a search party of those caves and he needs volunteers. Audrey Jane said that you and your sister were really good spelunkers."

"That's right," Ajay chimed in, the first time she opened her mouth since I arrived. "Ryan, Eden and I used to explore caves all the time near our home in Portland."

Technically, she wasn't lying. But for crying out loud! That was the Oregon Caves National Monument and it was with a tour guide on our elementary school's class trip! I swear, I wanted to strangle that girl!

Nick continued talking, unaware of the few words I mouthed to Ajay.

"WHAT THE HELL?"

She just smiled back, listening to Nick ramble on about the caves.

"So....like I said. These caves aren't your average limestone caves with stalactites and stuff. Yeah, they've got them, but these caves aren't one level. They all connect and there are quick drop-offs and cliffs inside them. It's a challenge for seasoned cave explorers. But the sheriff will be glad to have you join his group.

Got some volunteer firemen and road crew workers as well as local deputies. The rehearsal should be over in about an hour and a half. I told Ralph Hutchins to swing by and pick you guys up."

"Nick, I think you ought to know something. Eden, Audrey Jane and I---"

"I know. I know. You don't have to say anything. We're just darn lucky to have you on our crew."

Just then, the phone rang and Nick went to answer it. Ajay stepped outside and I followed her. Too bad I wasn't a cartoon character or she would have seen smoke coming out of my ears.

"Are you crazy? We could get killed in those caves!"

"It's the only way, Ryn. The only way to save my great- grandfather."

Then, for just a brief instant, I smelled something. And the stench was enough to gag a maggot. That primal, dead rot smell that meant time was about to flip-flop. Ajay gasped, but by the time she caught her breath, it was over.

"Maybe you're right," I said. But I knew this was one move that would put all of us between time and oblivion.

University of Missouri, Department of Geological Sciences
Office of Professor Howard Langston, Paleontological,
Sedimentological, and Stratigraphy Studies

Professor Howard Langston scrolled through his morning email, pausing every now and then to reach for his coffee. But when his eyes caught the message from Dr. Wesley Jamison's office at Texas A & M, Professor Langston jerked forward in his seat. His elbow caught the edge of the mug and knocked it to the ground.

But it wasn't until hours later that Professor Langston noticed the coffee stains on his tan khaki pants and sneakers.

Chapter Thirty-three:
Ryn

It was bad enough dealing with bossy, snappy and snarly Aeden for the past year. I thought things would get better when she turned 15, but boy, was I wrong! Now, I'm putting up with freaking self-absorbed, self-inflated Aeden. And she couldn't see past her stupid role in that play. I had just run after her as she left the ticket office and headed back to the Playhouse. Ralph Hutchins was still talking to Ajay and Nick.

"Aeden, stop walking and listen for once."

"I'm not going into those caves, Ryn. I need to work on my lines and for heaven's sakes, the choreography. My timing has to be precise. You've got Ajay. And all those other people."

"Don't forget you were the one who insisted we save Hank Clayton, or did you forget that already?"

I knew that last comment of mine stung her because she didn't say a word and I continued speaking.

"It's not just the Hank Clayton thing. Something's going on with the time-space continuum. We're getting glimpses of the Ice Age and I think we're going to find ourselves tumbling back there, like it or not. And Aeden, we need to be together. All three of us. Get it? It's the only way to ensure that when time makes a final flip, we get back to the 21st century."

"Maybe I'm not supposed to go back. Maybe I'm supposed to stay here and become famous."

"HOG CRAP! You can become famous, if that's what you need to do, when you get back to Portland. What about that calla lily play you were in? Maybe that's going to give you your big break."

"That's a high school play, Ryn. Not summer theater. Not summer theater with agents who come to scout out the talent."

"No one will be scouting out anything if you suddenly disappear in time. And believe me when I tell you, it's quite possible. Just picture yourself singing and dancing on stage and then, all of sudden, a stinking smell, darkness and no Aeden! Is it really worth the risk?"

My sister had the same look on her face that babies get when they've just dropped a binky or whatever you call those mouthy things. *Don't tell me you're about to cry, Aeden, because we don't have time for this.* Finally, she spoke.

"I'll go with you and Ajay to the caves, and I really hope we find Hank Clayton alive. But I'm not giving up my role in 'Brigadoon.' Not yet anyway."

"Fine, Aeden. Fine. Now go get whatever you need from your cabin because we're leaving with the sheriff in ten minutes."

I watched her storm off and shook my head. *I just hope we find him alive, too. And to hell with your theater career, Miss Hathaway!*

Chapter Thirty-four:
Darnell Legrun

Darnell knew that it happened in less than a blink. It had to. But that's not how it went. He could feel his finger pulling the trigger toward him. But the metal moved slowly as if it were stuck in some sort of resin or gel, forcing Darnell to exert even more pressure as he tried to steady his shaking hand. It had been a long time since Darnell had used a gun. And that was to hunt rabbits with his uncle. Back when Uncle L. J. was still single and had time for his nephew.

And then, a sound that blasted every nerve ending in his body. Darnell jolted and dropped the gun. As he bent down to reach for it, the blast echoed with such intensity that his stomach seemed to twist and turn. His hand moved across the dank cave floor. That gun had to be right there. But it didn't matter. He could always return with a flashlight. What mattered was the fact that Hank Clayton no longer posed a problem. Darnell was sure that the bullet pierced the back of the man's head. Proximity and aim saw to that. Then why didn't he hear the thud of a body falling to the ground?

"What the hell," he thought. "I'd better ditch

that truck someplace out of town and call Randy from a gas station or somewhere so I can get a ride home."

Turning to the cave entrance, Darnell began to walk quickly. Had he been in there so long that it was dark outside? Impossible. It took seconds to shoot Hank Clayton, not hours. He stumbled forward, trying to get a glimpse of whatever daylight was left and that's when he heard the rustling sound of water. Fast moving water. Darnell froze. He had been in these caves since he was a kid. Everyone in that part of Missouri had traipsed through them. But whatever waterways had once been a part of the Ice Age, they no longer existed in the 20th century. "Where," Darnell thought, "is that sound coming from? And why didn't I hear it before?"

He took a deep breath and continued to walk. This time, slowly, making sure that one foot touched solid ground before lifting the next. Certain that the entrance was a few yards ahead, Darnell kept moving forward, thankful that he had his cigarette lighter for a beacon. But when a sudden flash of light caught him unaware, he lost his footing and tripped over a small rock, tossing the lighter and landing hard on both knees. By the time he stood up, the flash and the lighter were gone. And so was his sense of direction.

Chapter Thirty-five:
Ajay

The sweatshirt I had taken from the cabin's pile of "cast and crew clothing" was scratchy and thin, but it was the only one there. Aeden had managed to find some sort of sweater and I wasn't paying attention to what Ryn was wearing. But I knew that caves were cold. Even if the ones I had explored in Oregon came with brochures and tour guides. I just wished that stupid sheriff had given each of us a flashlight instead of doling out the only one to Ryn. How sexist!

There were at least thirteen volunteers, not including us. But we were the only ones who were in this particular cave. Minutes before, Sheriff Hutchins had slapped Ryn on the back, giving him orders, or at least trying to sound as if he was.

"Seeing as you're experienced spelunkers, I guess you'll be fine searching together. Remember, if you come across a body, don't touch anything. Just come back to the car and wait."

I was furious. Everyone had already made up their minds that my great- grandfather was dead. I crossed my arms and stared at the sheriff.

"But what if Hank Clayton's still alive and hurt?"

"Then you tell him that help is on the way and all of you come back to the car like I said before. Do you understand?"

"Yeah," we seemed to say in unison as we headed into the largest of the cavern openings. The other volunteers were assigned to the smaller caves and had arrived way before us. The sheriff planned on joining them and walked with us only as far as our cave's entrance. Then he turned away but not before reminding us not to touch anything suspicious. Like that would ever cross my mind. I was still seething about the way he put Ryn in charge but didn't let on.

Aeden and I walked on either side of her brother following the dim beam of light until the path narrowed. Then we proceeded in single file with Ryn in front and Aeden in the back. Apparently I wasn't the only one in a bad mood. Ryn was really annoyed and Aeden couldn't stop grumbling.

"Quit shaking that flashlight all around. It's making us dizzy. Why don't you let me hold it and lead for a while?"

"Because you get all freaked out at stuff."

"Oh, and having you hold the flashlight is going to make things better?"

"At least I won't drop it if we come across some sort of animal or something."

"Is that the best flashlight they could have given us? It's so dim. I can hardly see."

"I don't have a degree in flashlights, Aeden, but I think this is the best they had in 1952 so deal with it!"

Aeden was right, though. The light was dim. And all we could see was rock wall and the beginnings of some stalactites and stalagmites. The pathway was getting more difficult for us and I could feel my feet slipping on the damp cave floor. I had to say something.

"I don't want to sound like a baby, but what if the flashlight batteries go dead?"

It was weird. Almost as if Ryn anticipated my question. He jumped at the response.

"I've got matches in my pockets. Lots of them. Took them from the Playhouse kitchen. Remember when we first got stuck in the Ice Age and couldn't make a fire? Well, that won't happen again."

I gulped.

"The Ice Age or the fire?"

But before Ryn could answer, I saw the shadow of a large figure just a few feet away.

And then, it suddenly seemed to topple over and disappear.

"Did you see that? Did you see that?"

I could hear myself screaming and I couldn't stop.

"Did you see that shadow? I swear, it was the shadow of a person and it just fell over. Disappeared. Flash your light at it, Ryn!"

"Calm down, Ajay, I saw it, too."

Ryn moved quickly to where the shadow was, waving the flashlight against both sides of the cavern wall.

"There's nothing here. Absolutely nothing."

But there was something. Another shadow had just appeared over Ryn's head. Only he didn't see it. The scream left my mouth automatically. And it echoed in the dank air of the cavern along with Aeden's shrieks.

It was the shadow of an animal, at least three times our size. And as Aeden and I watched it leap behind Ryn, we froze. We could see its mouth opening. Large enough that the fang had cast a dark image of its own against the rock wall.

"Run Ryn!" I yelled, but the words never left my mouth. They were garbled in fear and panic.

I stood there, helpless, alongside Aeden, expecting that beast to pounce on top of Ryn and tear off his flesh. But nothing happened. There was no beast. No saber-tooth tiger. Just an image. A remnant. My hands started to shake and I keep biting my lower lip.

"Did you see it? Did you see it?"

Aeden kept repeating herself as Ryn spun the flashlight above his head, illuminating the cave's ceiling.

"Get a grip, both of you," he yelled. "I caught a glimpse of it, too. But the animal isn't here. We're safe."

I took a step closer to the spot where Ryn was standing.

"Then where did it go? The shadow was right above your head."

"What we saw was an artifact. Not the real thing. Did either of you pick up a strange odor or feel the least bit dizzy just as the shadow appeared? Because what I'm thinking is that we witnessed a time rift. There was a saber-toothed tiger here all right, only not in present time. We got lucky. The time rift didn't grab us. It very well could have---"

And then he stopped speaking. He didn't need to continue. I knew what he was about to say so I finished the sentence for him.

"swallowed Hank Clayton back to the Ice Age."

Chapter Thirty-six:
Aeden

I threw my arms around Ajay and gave her a hug because I didn't know what else to do. We walked a bit further into the cave looking for any sign of a kidnapping, but the only thing I saw was the remains of a campfire. Probably one of many since kids hung out in these caves. For a minute it reminded me of Tom Sawyer and Becky Thatcher. They got lost in a Missouri cave. But they were fictional, too. Still... I shuddered as I made my way around one of the rock formations. The floor was getting slippery and the jutting rocks made it tough to maneuver around.

Then, without warning, my brother just stopped in his tracks inches in front of Ajay and she let him know about it.

"Geez Ryn, I almost tripped over you."

"Shh, listen. Do you hear that?"

The sounds were garbled and low but something about them made the small hairs on my arms stand up.

"Let's go back, Ryn. We haven't found anything and this is creeping me out."

Ajay didn't need any convincing. She was one step away from a full blown panic attack.

"Aeden's right. Just turn around and let's go. GO NOW. I MEAN IT RYN!"

But Ryn just stood there, waving the flashlight around the open spaces between the stalactites while Ajay just kept yelling "NOW! NOW!"

"Cool it, Ajay and listen. Those sounds are voices. Can you hear them?"

Ajay stopped bellowing and I forced myself to listen; but all I could hear were muffled sounds. Grunting sounds. And then I had an awful thought.

"Ryn, what if we're hearing the sounds of that cat? That tiger? Could time have brought it forward? Oh my God, Ryn. We've got to get the hell out of here. Now!"

He started to move, but not towards the cave entrance.

"Tigers don't make grunting sounds. And they're light-footed. Whatever's making that noise isn't a saber-tooth tiger. Get a grip."

I wanted to yank that flashlight out of his hand and start running, but you don't run in caves, especially damp ones where your footing really matters. And then there was Ajay. Ajay was on the verge of hysteria now. If I started to make a quick move, she'd be a raving maniac.

"So you want us to do what, Ryn? Just stand here and wait?"

"Aeden, Ajay—it's not just the sound. Take a look. Light is coming from behind those larger rocks. And it's wavy."

"My God!" I could hear myself shriek. "We're going back in time."

Ajay grabbed my wrist and pressed in with her nails. I was too numb to do anything about it. And then I heard Ryn laugh. Not a bellicose uproarious laugh, but one of those smart aleck sounds he started making way back in middle school.

"No, we're not rippling back. Everything else is stable. It's got to be the flashlights from the other search party. Remember, these caves connect. Look, you two. And listen."

It was voices, all right. But not anyone talking. More like everyone screaming. Flashlight beams seems to be coming from every direction. It took me a few seconds to process what I was hearing and when I did, I was too stunned with fear to move. The other search party had seen something and it wasn't a body. Whatever it was, it made them forget about any protocol they had learned for walking in caves.

"Run! Run for your lives!"

"Get out! Get out NOW!"

"Hurry! Run! Fast"

"Quick!" Ryn said as he shoved Ajay and me against the nearest wall. "Just stay pressed against this wall and let them run. If we try to out race them, we'll be trampled."

I knew it made sense but was that worse than what they were running from? I was surprised at how calmly I spoke.

"Shouldn't we be running, too, Ryn?"

"They're going to fall. It's way too slippery. And they're panicking. That means they'll be breaking the stalactites and when those fall, they can kill you. Just stay still."

Ryn was right. A few people fell but they managed to get up. And no one noticed us. They just kept running and pushing at each other. Flashlight beams bounced off of every wall. And then I heard a loud, cracking sound followed by a dull thud. Ryn shook my arm.

"What did I tell you? It's stalactites falling. Too many of them and this whole cave could give way. We don't have a choice. We've got to go out the way they came in."

"You're crazy!" Ajay screamed. "Crazy! You want to run right into whatever scared the crap out of volunteer deputies and firefighters?"

And then, another thud. Only this one echoed and echoed in the darkness. I reached out and held Ajay's hand.

"I don't like this either. But we can't go back the way we came. Come on, Ryn. Just shine the light and we'll find the entrance those other guys used. Well, what are you waiting for?"

"Don't start screaming but I am shining the light. Only....the bulb just blew."

Chapter Thirty-seven: *Marcy Meadows*

Marcy slammed the door to the ticket office and spoke before Nick could even turn around.

"So now what are we supposed to do? Everyone went off with the sheriff to search the caves for some kidnapped guy and the rehearsal just fizzled. Like that. Done. We'll never be ready for opening night."

"Calm down. You get like this every summer and everything always works out."

"Not this time. We lost one of our leads and the understudy just joined that search team. Plus, I have no idea how she'll be in front of an audience. Rehearsal is one thing. A live audience is the other. And I've got to perform, too. This is my big chance. Those agents from back east aren't going to give us more than one chance."

"Like I said…"

"You're not listening, Nick. There's other stuff, too. Weird stuff. Like finding blood and some strange animal remains on one of our props, and that storm, what the heck was that? People are talking. Something fishy is going on."

"So now you're worried because Missouri weather is unpredictable and some poor raccoon or something wandered into the Playhouse and got fried on the lights? If you were going to worry about something, try the theft of five grand. Maybe next year we can do an Ancient Greek tragedy amphitheater style since our roof will be completely shot by then! "

Marcy quickly shoved her hands into the pockets of her jeans so Nick wouldn't notice them shaking.

"I'm sure you'll get your money."

"Yeah, how can you be so sure?"

"Maybe someone just needed to borrow it for a little while."

"Honestly, Marcy, with an imagination like that, you should be writing plays, not acting in them."

"I'm sorry if I upset you, Nick. I didn't mean to rattle your cage. Anyway, I've got to see Clarisse about some last minute changes. Do you know where she is?"

"Yeah. At least that's one mystery I can solve today. Clarisse borrowed the truck to go into town. She said she needed to pick up some last minute supplies. I'm surprised she didn't say anything to you."

"Me, too. Anyway, I'd better get back to the stage. If the sheriff comes back with any news about anything, please let me know, OK?"

"Sure thing, Marcy."

Nick turned back to the paperwork on his desk as Marcy quietly closed the door behind her and pulled out a cigarette from the top pocket of her shirt. She had flipped open her small lighter so many times that it had become automatic. Only this time, her hands were shaking so hard that she just tossed the cigarette on the ground and kept walking.

Chapter Thirty-eight:
Ryn

*E*ven in the dark, Ajay managed to find my arm and give it a yank as she yelled.

"Strike a match, Ryn. You said you had matches. Strike one!"

"That's not going to help us. It'll go out too fast. We need to make some sort of torch in order to light our way. Remember Aeden? The torches from the Bastille? And the sewers? They lasted forever."

"Yeah, but there are no torches hanging from the walls here. So now what?"

"We make one. We already have something to start a fire. And we can tear off a piece of our clothing for the cloth part of it. We just need some wood, like a branch, or maybe even a bone. Did either of you notice anything like that on the ground?"

"Nope," Ajay said. "All I noticed were these stupid rocks. I'm surprised one of them didn't fall on me. And I'm not about to tear off any of my clothes. You can tear yours."

But Aeden had seen something.

"Old campfires, Ryn. This must be a popular hide-out for the local kids. There was one just a few feet back."

"OK, look. Suppose I light just one match and hold it out for you. Do you think you can make your way back and grab a long piece of firewood? Maybe one that hadn't burnt yet. Or, you hold the match and I'll go back."

I've got to admit that Aeden was a hell of lot braver since the Bastille. I mean, up until that point, I couldn't even get her to go into the funhouse at a carnival. Maybe there's hope for her yet. I held out the match and watched her walk back a ways, darting in and out of the few stalactites that remained. Then Ajay started in.

"Do you think the place will cave in? Hurry up, Aeden!"

"Don't hurry," I yelled as I poked Ajay in the elbow. "Go slow. Take short steps and try not to disturb anything."

I could see her bending down to grab something when my thumb started to burn and I dropped the match.

"Hold on," I yelled. "I'll light another one. Stay put!"

I reached into my pocket, expecting to find a few matchbooks, but all I found was one matchbook and a small hole in the pocket. The others must have slipped out.

Ajay couldn't help but notice me stalling.

"What happened? What's going on?"

"Nothing. Calm down. I'm just getting a match."

I opened the cover and could feel three matches. I had to use one for Aeden. That meant only two tries to get the torch going. Then I remembered something. Torches need to be dipped in oil or animal fat. Crap! Even cavemen knew that. And where was I going to find oil?

"Come on, Ryn,"

I could hear my sister's voice.

"Light the darn thing so I can get back."

I sighed and lit the match. Then I watched as Aeden walked back towards us holding a narrow branch of some sort.

"Useless," I thought to myself. "This is all useless without something to dip the torch material into."

I was about to say something when Ajay spoke and everything changed.

"My lip is bleeding. I bit it when we saw that image. That shadow. Well, anyway, I need to put some chapstick on it or it will just keep bleeding. Hold on."

I couldn't believe my ears.

"Chapstick? You've got chapstick? Don't waste it on your lips!"

"What? What you mean don't put it on my lips? They're all cut and dry!"

"I need that chapstick, Ajay. We all do. We've got to rub it on the piece of material for the torch. I forgot that torches need oil."

"Well my lips need moisturizer!"

Then she let out a long sigh.

"Fine. I'll just use a little bit and then you can have it."

I swear, Lady Gaga didn't take as much time putting on her makeup. Ajay handed me the chapstick just as I finished tearing off the sleeve of my shirt. Then, I wrapped the fabric around the wooden branch and tore two ends off so that I could tie them and secure it. Next, I began to rub the thick sticky stuff all over the fabric.

"Are you sure this is going to work?" Aeden asked.

"Absolutely. Just hold on to it and watch."

I lit the first of the last two matches and held it close to the material. It started to catch immediately and just as I was about to say something, it burnt out. Just like that.

"Well, light another match," Ajay said. "You've got lots of them."

I wanted to tell them the truth but decided to wait and see. If the match ignited the cloth and stayed lit, then there was no need to panic them.

If not, well, I just braced myself for the screams that were sure to follow.

A slight tremor made my hand feel as if someone else was moving it. Slowly, I lit the match and moved it towards the cloth. Only this time I moved it all around so it would ignite more than one area. Then, I held my breath and waited.

It worked! The torch worked! And it lit up the area with far more intensity than the old flashlight. We could see well into the cave. And in that instant, I regretted ever having lit it in the first place.

Chapter Thirty-nine: Darnell Legrun

*T*he sound of rushing water seemed to surround him as Darnell stood up and tried to focus in the dark. The cave was as black as pitch and he cursed under his breath for dropping the lighter and losing it. The entrance couldn't be too far back, he thought, as he stretched his arms out in front, making sure he wouldn't bump into one of the lower hanging stalactites. But which way was the entrance? There was nothing to guide him. Still, Darnell figured he'd better keep moving in one direction. If that didn't bring him closer to the entrance, he'd turn around and try the other way. He didn't even want to think about making left or right turns. Four options and all of them stunk.

"Damn that stupid Randy," he muttered. "When I get out of here I'm really going to nail it to him."

His feet moved slowly and deliberately on the damp ground. It was impossible to tell where the water was coming from but the sounds got louder as if something or someone had angered the currents in the water.

"This can't be right," Darnell whispered to himself, afraid to say it out loud. "Got to turn my butt around and go the other way."

He was careful to make a complete turn and start to backtrack to his original position. Still, the water seemed to surround him, making Darnell wonder if he wasn't walking parallel to some sort of stream or channel. But he didn't remember one when he entered the cave with Hank Clayton. In fact, he never came across any water in all the years that he and his school buddies had traipsed through the caves, looking for a good spot to sit and drink the beers that someone had lifted from their parents' house.

Then Darnell began to wonder if he hadn't inadvertently found his way to a lower level in the cave, one that he hadn't explored. But he dismissed that thought, reminding himself that he stayed on level ground when he forced Hank Clayton into the cavern. The sounds had to be his mind playing tricks on him. Darnell remembered reading somewhere that people who are forced into sensory deprivation situations begin to imagine all sorts of things. So maybe that's what was happening to him.

"Gotta keep my mind straight," he said as he began to count the steps, figuring that if he didn't see moonlight from the cave's entrance after 100 steps, he would need to turn around and then pick a new direction. Left or right. Fifty-fifty chance. By now Darnell was getting agitated and his heartbeat seemed to intensify.

Easy does it. What's the worst thing that can happen? I'm stuck here all night? Big fat hairy deal. The sun will come up and I'll find the entrance. Just gotta worry that no one gets to the truck before then.

He remembered counting 100 steps. But how many before that? And where did he leave off? His hands began to shake and he clenched his fists. *Just gotta pick a direction and move.*

Go backwards. Gotta go backwards. Then left or right. Just move.

Darnell could have sworn he was not alone in the cave. The hell! It had to be that sensory deprivation crap, he thought. Or maybe someone found the truck and they were tracking him. Whatever the case, he had to keep moving. Inhaling slowly, Darnell was about to turn when a deep musky smell burned his nostrils and lingered in the air.

Damn it! Someone's in this cave. Someone who overdid it with the cheap men's cologne. But the smell intensified and turned fecal.

"What the-----" Darnell started to say, but he never finished. As he reached his hand out to make sure there were no obstacles, his fingertips touched the coarse hairs on the bear's face. The creature had approached him so slowly, so quietly, that by the time Darnell realized what was about to happen, even if he had his gun, it would have been too late.

Chapter Forty:
Councilman Barkley

Noreen Brown quickly finished touching up her lips and snapped the lid of the compact closed just as Clarence Barkley entered his campaign headquarters. "Bob Barkley," as he preferred to be known, was even more short tempered that afternoon than usual and it meant that Noreen would be staying late at work for her boss. The third time this week. He lashed out at everyone in the room before she could even utter a greeting.

"How come I'm driving around this town seeing signs up for my opponent but not any of my own? Where are they? What's going on?"

Noreen pressed her lips together and walked quickly over to where he was standing. The room had gotten so quiet that the click of her heels could be heard on the wooden floor.

"They'll be available shortly. We just picked up the wood from the lumberyard the other day."

"Make sure every highway, every roadway and every alleyway has one."

Noreen nodded as she looked around the room. Paid workers and the few volunteers immediately buried themselves in paperwork or started to pick up the phones.

"And that's another thing," Bob Barkley went on, "no personal phone calls. This isn't a coffee klatch."

Noreen didn't need to be reminded about the phones. Her predecessor had lost her job over personal calls and Noreen wasn't about to let that happen to her.

"We need to go over your schedule for appearances, Mr. Barkley. The local chapter for the League of Women Voters wants to hold a debate."

Bob Barkley sighed. He was about to respond with an off-hand, flippant remark but at the last second, thought better of it.

"Just schedule the thing. You know my calendar better than I do."

Just then, one of the workers shouted from across the room.

"Councilman Barkley, it's the newspaper. They want to know your opinion about the missing highway commissioner and those surveyors who got tied up."

Bob Barkley could feel a slight flush in his cheeks as he opened the door to his office.

"I'll be at my desk and I'll answer the call from there. Put the line on hold."

"Yes, sir," the young male worker responded, eager to remain in Bob Barkley's good graces.

Noreen positioned herself near the file cabinets just outside the councilman's private office. And even with the door closed, she could hear one end of the conversation – a well-rehearsed, political response if ever there was one.

"Like all the good citizens in our county, I am deeply concerned about the safety of Commissioner Hank Clayton and will extend all of my support to the sheriff and local authorities."

With the receiver still pressed against his ear, Bob Barkley pushed down on the two plastic knobs at the base of the phone, ending the call. Then, he quickly dialed another number. Only this time Noreen didn't hear the conversation. Someone needed her assistance and she couldn't linger near the file drawers. She only heard two words - Hank Clayton.

Chapter Forty-one:
Ajay

Ryn stretched out his arm, blocking me from taking another step. It was the same thing my mother did when she was driving and had to brake suddenly. But this wasn't the street and there wasn't another car in front of us.

"My God," Aeden whispered from behind. "It's that bear. That cave bear. Oh my God. Either we've gone back in time or something brought him into this century."

"Walk back slowly," Ryn said as he held out the torch. "He's afraid of the fire. He'll leave us alone."

I wanted to say something but the words froze in my mouth and I stumbled backwards, narrowly missing a large rock. Aeden had grabbed my shoulder so I wouldn't fall.

"He's not moving back, Ryn. The bear is not moving away."

"You and Ajay need to take slow steps backwards. I'll keep moving forward with the torch. Just move slowly. No sudden movements."

"No sudden movements." Isn't that what they say when a bomb is about to go off? Maybe

it's the catch phrase for kiss your you-know-what good-bye because nothing is going to save you. We're going to die. In a cave. A pre-historic cave. I don't want to die a grizzly death. I want to die in my sleep when I'm older than a hundred and even then I'm not so sure.

If my body did move at all, I don't know how. My mind seemed to spin and all I could see was that giant animal standing a few feet from Ryn. Then, Ryn did something I never expected. He lunged at the bear, thrusting the torch straight ahead and making so much noise that it actually echoed.

This might work. It does in the movies. Oh my God. Make it work. Oh my God.

I kept my eyes on the bear so I never noticed what Aeden was doing. I figured she was taking small steps backwards. But something went wrong, because the next thing I knew, I heard her scream. But not a full scream. The kind of scream you start but never get to finish because someone put their hand over your mouth.

But the scream must have scared the bear. Or maybe the heat from the torch had gotten too close, because that monster of a thing turned and wandered into a small opening. Ryn was still watching it as he spoke.

"It's OK, Aeden. You can stop yelling. The bear's gone. He went into a small opening. Look. See for yourself."

Then he moved the torch in front of the spot where the bear had been, only there was no longer an opening. Just solid rock wall.

"Something must have triggered a time ripple because that bear slipped back to his own time. OK, Aeden?"

But Aeden couldn't hear us. She was no longer there.

My voice came back in spurts. Soft and raspy one second. Loud and uncontrollable the next.

"She's gone, Ryn. Gone. She was right here. Right behind me. Please don't tell me that she's now someplace else in time. I am going to freak-out."

"Stand absolutely still and don't move."

He walked quietly to where I was standing and with the torch in his hand, looked down. I could hear him take a deep breath.

"It's an opening, Ajay. The ground gave way. All that running when everyone panicked must have weakened an already unstable spot in the cave. Aeden's not in another time, just a different place. She's fallen into the cavern below this one. Whatever you do, stay still. There's no way of knowing how deep it goes."

"In the movies, they throw the torch down and find out how far down it goes."

"This isn't 'Journey to the Center of the Earth,' Ajay, but you've got a point. I just need to light something small and toss it."

The next thing I knew, Ryn pried off a tiny piece of wood from the torch base and lit it. We leaned over and watched as it made its way down the opening. And that's when I realized he was right. This wasn't like the movies. Even though we could see the flame flickering below us, we had no way of knowing how far down it had gone. Or if Aeden was still alive.

I felt my throat tighten as the flame disappeared. I hadn't been around Ryn and Aeden for years, but in the few days that I was with them, it was obvious that Ryn would never leave his sister behind. And that scared the living daylights out of me because it meant he was about to jeopardize his own life, and possibly mine.

Chapter Forty-two:
Hank Clayton

*T*he sheriff's search party thundered out of the cave as if they were running from a swarm of bees. The ten or so volunteers didn't slow down until they reached the cars that were parked in front of the caverns.

Ralph Hutchins had just finished radioing a report to the state police when he looked up and saw the commotion. In an instant, he was out of his car with his hand pressing against his gun.

"Whoa. Slow down! What on earth are you all doing? Did you find anything?"

But instead of getting a coherent response, all Ralph Hutchins heard was a jumble of words.

"Kill it! Kill it!"

"Giant bear!"

"Horrific!"

"It's right behind us!"

"Cave. Bear. Get your guns!"

Taking a step forward, Ralph stretched out his arms and motioned for everyone to calm down.

"There ain't a single thing behind you. No bear. No nothing. And we've never had reports of bears in these caves. Now can someone, just one person, tell me what's going on?"

A tall, balding man in his late thirties rubbed the top of his forehead and spoke.

"There was a bear in that cave, but not the likes of any Missouri bears. It was enormous. Towered over us as if we were about to be his next meal. No time to do anything but run."

"And no sign of Hank Clayton?"

"Sheriff," one of the firemen said, "Hank Clayton, if he was in that cavern, may have been the bear's last meal. I don't think we're a rescue party anymore. Just a ----"

"Don't say it," someone else shouted.

Ralph Hutchins could see that the group was unnerved. Unnerved and a short step from the kind of stress that puts people in hospitals. He knew better than to press them any further.

"Look, all of you take a breath and calm down. Is everyone back from the cave?"

As he spoke, he looked at the crowd and realized that the three spelunkers from the Playhouse were missing.

"Stay put, everyone. We may have a problem."

Chapter Forty-three:
Aeden

It was instinctive and automatic. My feet moved backwards as I stared at the large beast in front of us. He seemed paralyzed by the flame at the tip of the torch, but for how long? I don't even remember breathing, just taking slow steps. And then, my foot slipped and there was no ground beneath it.

My whole body slid into the darkness before I could finish yelling for help. But it wasn't like tumbling into a hole. Not like "Alice in Wonderland." I was falling but my arms were scraping against rocks. I must have been against the side wall of the opening. At first the rocks tore into my skin like tiny razors. But as I kept falling, the sensation on my skin got softer, like sand. The composition of the cave had changed.

When I landed, it was on sandy ground, and other than the cuts and bruises that stung my arms, the rest of my body felt fine. I stood up and tilted my head back, trying to see the light from Ryn's torch. A tiny flickering thing that looked like a firefly seemed to float out of nowhere and disappear.

"Can you hear me?" I screamed. "I'm down here."

I thought I heard something but it was impossible to tell. The cavern had sounds of its own. Trickling sounds, hollow sounds and the kinds of sounds that can't really be explained in words. I tried again.

"I'm down here! Can you hear me?"

At first I thought my eyes were getting use to the dark, but then I realized that I was seeing a soft hue of light in the distance. It was an opening. A way out. But without my brother and Ajay, I wasn't about to find out.

The trickling sounds seemed to be coming from the other side of the wall. A waterfall maybe? Or a stream? I had no way of knowing. But the fact that the cave had more than one level frightened me to death. If I were to slip again, then where would I be? And could someone find me?

I stood absolutely still, took a deep breath and screamed at the top of my lungs.

"Ryn! Ajay! Down here!"

It looked like a pinpoint way above my head, but I swore it was the light from that torch. Someone had heard me. Then why couldn't I hear them?

Chapter Forty-four:
Darnell Legrun

The bear's claw ripped into Darnell's face as the animal tried to brush the man aside. But Darnell froze, too numb to process what was happening. Again, the bear swiped at the man's face and chin, this time gouging Darnell's neck before turning around and lumbering off.

Darnell Legrun stumbled and staggered. His mind was no longer in control of his feet. And when his toes landed hard against the side of a rock, he fell forward and plunged into the fast moving stream that was cutting its way through the cave.

The icy water seemed to shock every part of his body as he tried to fight the current and reach for the stream's embankment. It was impossible. The water was too fast and Darnell's senses were slowing down. Blood had congealed and pasted over one of his eyes. Darnell was sure that the bear had ripped part of the outer skin. But in the darkness, with the water rushing at him, it made little difference.

At first he flailed his arms, partly out of fear but mostly because it was an unconscious reaction to the water. But it was his legs that would ultimately betray him. They were heavy and cumbersome. And the boots he was wearing, along with thick jeans, didn't allow for any movement in the water. It seemed as if the current was moving faster and faster, and even though Darnell managed to control the motion in his arms, the effort was futile.

He couldn't take in enough air through his nose and had to inhale using his mouth. But the force of the water coming at him filled his mouth with liquid, sludge and grit. If he spit it out, he couldn't catch his breath, and if he kept it in, he felt as if he would suffocate. It was a fight Darnell was going to lose. Still, he tried to move his arms to reach for anything – a ledge, a wall, something. He had to maneuver himself against the edge of the stream and try to hang on to the rock wall. But where? And more importantly, how?

Darnell had become part of the stream itself, just like the sand, rock, and animal debris that defined it. His body was getting weaker and he had no idea how long he'd been trapped in the current. Minutes? Hours? The absolute lack of light played tricks on his mind as he lapsed in and out of consciousness. And the effort it took to move his arms was Herculean.

Was it his imagination or was the current getting stronger? As Darnell struggled to keep his head above the water, the stream widened and made a quick twist to the left. A small eddy had formed, trapping animal bones, detritus, fecal matter, and sand. A solid limestone wall framed the whirlpool. In the instant it took for Darnell to inhale, the current pushed him against the rock wall, banging his head with such force that the water began to turn red. Not a slow oozing of color, but a fast change. There was no stopping the blood.

The last image that came to Darnell's mind was fragmented. He was certain he had seen a light and heard voices, but a grey murkiness overtook him and shut down his senses. His body was trapped in the whirlpool, along with time itself.

Chapter Forty-five:
Ryn

The sounds were faint and muffled, but I swore it was my sister. Ajay and I would have no choice but to plunge into that hole ourselves and get to her. But with no ropes or any means to lower ourselves, it was like a step off a cliff. And what moron does that? Yet, that was exactly what I had in mind.

"Ajay, this cavern has levels. And if we don't get to Aeden, we might never have that chance."

"So what are you saying? We just jump in?"

"Not exactly. I can set the torch down so it leans over the edge while I lower you with my arms. There must be rock lips or small ledges you can reach. From there, you'll be able to make your way down. Then I'll follow."

"What about the torch?"

"We won't be able to take it, but maybe there's a light source below. And if not, then we'll find a way for all three of us to climb back up."

I knew I was lying. I knew there was no way in hell we'd get back up, but if I told Ajay the truth, she'd never agree to going down that opening. And all of us needed to stay together.

"Are you sure?"

"Positive."

I choked on my own lie.

"I hate this, Ryn. I really hate this."

"I know. I know. Just come on."

Ajay took a deep breath and leaned over the hole.

"My God. It looks endless."

"It just appears that way because of the darkness. Don't look down. Just get on your knees slowly and put your feet over the edge. I won't let go of your arms."

Trust is usually something that's earned over time. But once in a while, under duress or strain, it's there. Like the moment Ajay took my arms and started down the hole.

"I've got to let go of you. Can you grab onto anything?"

"Just let go of one hand and I'll see."

Slowly, I released her right hand.

"Oh no. Damn! Damn! Damn! Damn!"

"What? What happened Ajay?"

"My fingernails are getting little bits of rock in them. Do you know how long it's going to take to ever have them look good again?"

Fingernails. The girl is worried about her fingernails. Unbelievable. We're in a cave in another decade with no way of knowing if we'll get out, and Ajay is worried about her stupid fingernails?

I had all I could do to keep myself from screaming. But then I realized that if Ajay was concerned about her manicure, she wasn't about to panic or freak out. Her nails were keeping her focused.

"Just keep going," I yelled.

With the torch against the lip edge of the hole, I could see the top of Ajay's head slowing disappearing into the darkness.

"Are you all right?"

"Yeah."

And that was the last thing I heard.

Chapter Forty-six:
Clarisse

larisse pulled the theater truck into the Playhouse drive and headed for the kitchen. It was late afternoon and she hadn't heard any news about the search party. The local radio station had issued an "All-Call" for volunteers to assist the sheriff's office and she knew immediately that her brother would respond. Andy was always such a softie when it came to those things. That was just one of the reasons why everyone liked him. And why they were willing to help him out when things went amuck at his farm.

The late winter frost and the early torrential rains had all but destroyed his crops. But the feed corn was still a possibility. Only now, the harvester had broken and was beyond repair. Andy had managed to secure a bank loan to purchase a new machine, but the funds wouldn't be available for another three weeks, and that would be too late.

"Can't someone loan you the money until the bank comes through?" Clarisse had asked him when she stopped by his farm after practice a few days ago.

"I asked Lon Percy at the lumberyard. Usually he's willing to spot me the money. But he acted so strange. So distant. Almost scared. So I left it alone."

"Don't worry. Something will turn up."

"Yeah, the foreclosure papers for the property."

Clarisse thought about that conversation as she swung the door open to the kitchen. Marcy and a few of the cast members were eating cold meat loaf with bread. Marcy looked up from her plate when she saw Clarisse.

"Just cold meat loaf tonight. Where were you? You didn't say anything about needing supplies."

"It was just a few odds and ends. Besides, the rehearsal was over the minute the sheriff's search started."

"Are you sure that's all it was, odds and ends?"

"What are you saying, Marcy?"

"Nothing. Sorry. It's just that so many strange things are happening."

Clarisse put a slice of the meatloaf on a paper plate and began to pick at it with a fork.

"Marcy, if you found out that someone was in trouble, really big trouble, and they just needed you to kind of do something illegal, even though they didn't actually ask you, but you knew that no one was going to get hurt, and that everything would be straightened out in a little while, would you?"

Marcy reached across the table for a glass of water, and then thought better of it. What if Clarisse saw that slight tremor? It would be more obvious with a glass full of water. She cleared her throat and spoke quietly.

"I would expect people to understand. Especially friends. Sometimes we make decisions based on the overall good and not just the thing that seems right to do at that moment. So... er....Clarisse, what made you ask that in the first place?"

"Nothing in particular. It's just that everything is so tense around this Playhouse lately. I just get the feeling that someone is hiding something."

"You mean about the money? Or the kidnapping?"

"Or maybe something different altogether. Anyway, forget I said anything. I'm just over-tired, that's all."

"I understand. Better eat some dinner now while there's still meatloaf. Otherwise it's peanut butter and jelly."

Clarisse nodded as Marcy started to clear the table.

"I've got to review some stage notes. I'll see you later."

"OK," Clarisse said, still poking her food with a fork. "The show will be OK. The cast is pretty solid, even with the understudy."

"It has to be. It may be our last season."

Chapter Forty-seven:
Aeden

The sharp pain from getting kicked in the forehead stunned me for a second as I backed up. But not far enough. Ajay landed on me like a sack of rocks and we both fell into the soft sand.

"Ajay! You heard me! You're here! The ground just sort of opened up and I fell through. Are you OK?"

"I guess so. We'd better get out of the way. Your brother's coming down."

Then, she realized the same thing I did. There was light in the distance. An opening. An exit.

"As soon as Ryn's feet touch the ground, I'm heading directly for that light. We can get the heck out of here. What's taking him so long?"

I wondered the same thing. If Ryn was directly behind Ajay, then he should have landed by now. Ajay kept talking.

"Maybe the torch got in his way or something."

"Or maybe it's just taking him longer because there's no one up there to help."

"You don't suppose that bear came back?"

I knew my brother.

"If that bear came back, he would have scared it again and just jumped in. No, I think he's just taking his time. Hold on, Ajay."

But I was worried. In the semi-darkness, time seems to go slower than usual. And fear seems to spring out of nowhere. I was about to say something when I heard the crinkling sound of sand as something hard skidded on it.

"Ryn! You're here! What took you so long?"

"Gee, Aeden. I don't know. No one told me this was a race. My fingers kept slipping off of the rocks. All that limestone just peels away. Maybe you can register a complaint with the state. Will that make you happy?"

Ajay took a step forward and chimed in.

"She was just worried about you, Ryn. I mean, that bear could have come back."

"Thanks for not leaving me alone," I muttered.

"No problem. Now can we start finding a way out of here?"

Then it dawned on my brother.

"We can see each other! There's light. We don't need a torch. We just have to follow the light."

Ajay started to scurry ahead but Ryn grabbed the sleeve of her shirt.

"Go slowly. Walk softly. This level may be porous, too, and there may be other holes."

None of us said anything. We just inched our way through the cave. There were fewer obstacles on this level, just some larger stalactites and stalagmite ledges. But the cavern wall took on a phosphorus hue and sparked in the shadows.

"Oh my gosh," Ajay said as we got closer to it. "There's something jutting out of it."

Sure enough, it was a piece of cloth. A pattern I recognized. It was a red and white checkered cloth, like those tablecloths you see at Italian restaurants. But it was stuck. Fused into the rock wall itself. And that meant only one thing. Like us, it was trapped in time.

But it wasn't a tablecloth. Ryn reached out, touched it and gasped.

"It's the sleeve of a shirt. And we know who it belongs to. We all saw it. Hank Clayton was wearing a red and white checkered shirt the day he gave us a lift to the Playhouse. He must have been wearing the same shirt when he was kidnapped. Someone took him to these caves, all right. But time took him elsewhere."

Ajay took a loud, deep breath.

"You're saying he----"

Ryn paused for a moment. He does that when he's caught between saying what he thinks and trying to be diplomatic.

"We know there's a time loop to the Ice Age. I think your great-grandfather may have just found it."

Chapter Forty-eight:
Ryn

I held my breath, counting the seconds. It took eight. Eight seconds for Ajay to start wailing.

"He's trapped in the Ice Age? Is that what you're saying? Oh my God!"

"Before you start screaming like a banshee, listen a minute. It could very well be that your great-grandfather is still alive. At this moment anyway. It's just that he's at the other end of the time spectrum."

"So, go get him! Go get him!"

The last time I heard words like that, it was at some football game and the entire cheerleading squad was shouting them. Yay team. As I took a breath, Aeden tried to reason with Ajay.

"It's not that simple. I mean, we only time traveled twice, and one of those times it took us to two places. To get to your great-grandfather, we'd have to do the process again. From here. In this cave. And we'd need light, prisms, something to reflect..."

"And there's no guarantee where that'll take us," I added.

Then Ajay started crying. Something she must have mastered while still in the womb.

"I'm going to have nightmares the rest of my life, just seeing that red and white checkered sleeve in the rock."

Much as I hated to say it, I was going to have nightmares, too. I mean, it was beyond creepy. It was Stephen King creepy and that's why I knew we had to come back to the cave. I wasn't going to spend the rest of my life in analysis. The school counselors are getting pretty sick of me as it is.

"OK, Ajay, here's the deal. We've got to exit this cave and get back to the sheriff's cars. We'll tell them that we didn't find anything. Then, early tomorrow, before anyone gets up, we'll get back here. Only this time with reflective glass and a decent flashlight."

Aeden jumped in immediately.

"There are all sorts of glass animals in the prop room for 'The Glass Menagerie.' The glass swan, the little bunny, the fancy---"

"Oh my God, Aeden, I don't need the freaking prop list. Just sneak in there and grab a few of them when we get back. I'll get a flashlight from the kitchen and plenty of matches."

Ajay stopped crying long enough to ask how we would get back here.

"I'll have to borrow the Playhouse truck. Hopefully, we'll get it back before anyone notices." *Otherwise I can add 'grand theft auto' to my college resume.* "Now come on, we'd better get going. Everyone's probably back by now and waiting for us."

The exit was an easy one. We followed the light to a round opening just above the ground. From outside the cave, it would have gone unnoticed as a small hole. All of us managed to shimmy up by grabbing the small rock ledges. Even Ajay did it without too much complaining. Last time I tried something like that, it was in Paris and a heavy grate blocked the exit. Ajay never would have made it.

As I dusted myself off and looked across the small field to the parking lot, I could see the crowd of volunteers huddled near the sheriff's cars. And then I remembered something. The bear. What were we going to tell them about the bear?

Chapter Forty-nine:
Hank Clayton

*O*wen Masterson spotted the three kids when he turned his neck to swat at a mosquito.

"Look! It's those three spelunkers! They're OK!"

The sheriff immediately started waving and motioning for Ryn, Aeden and Ajay to get over to the vehicles. As soon as they were in ear-shot, he began talking.

"I suppose the three of you are going to tell me the same story about a giant bear."

Ryn quickly whispered to the girls. "Don't say anything. I've got this." Then he started laughing as he approached the sheriff.

"That poor little brown bear. We must have scared the crap out of it. Didn't you see that it was just a weird reflection that kept bouncing off of the rock formations? I swear to God, it made that thing look at least 10 feet tall! It scurried away as all of you were running out. Must have a den in there or something."

Everyone seemed to get quiet all at once. And then, they started talking.

"Scared the living bejesus out of me!"

"I could have sworn the thing was colossal!"

"Light? Reflecting off of it? Unbelievable. Whew!"

Ralph Hutchins motioned for everyone to quit talking.

"All right. All right. Now that that's settled, did you three find any evidence of Hank Clayton?"

"No, nothing," Ryn said as the girls nodded in agreement.

"We'll see if we can get a larger search crew by the weekend. Meanwhile, stay out of the cavern. Even little brown bears can be dangerous, especially if they've got young. Been going in and out of these caves for decades and no sign of bears. Maybe the thing migrated from somewhere. So steer clear until the weekend. And Owen, as soon as you get back, call a tow company will you? No sense leaving this stolen vehicle here."

"Sure thing, sheriff."

"Again – stay out of these caves everyone!"

He didn't have to ask twice. Even if Goldilocks herself offered to venture in there, none of the volunteers would have followed.

Chapter Fifty:
Ajay

We piled into the back of the sheriff's car and didn't say a word. One of the deputies sat in front and kept mumbling about the bear.

"Honest, Boss. I feel like such a dope. It was just a small brown bear."

"Relax. Apparently, the illusion scared the daylights out of everyone, not just you. The good thing is that no one got hurt. The bad thing is that...well, we've got to continue the search this weekend."

Aeden suddenly came to life but she wasn't thinking about bears.

"The play opens this weekend. Friday night is opening night."

"She's right, Boss," the deputy continued. "That cast and crew is going to be too tied up to spare volunteers."

"Calm down, we'll just notify the locals and neighboring communities."

I glanced at Ryn. If he and Aeden were right, we'd find my great- grandfather in the morning. But Aeden was beginning to worry me. She was getting really obsessed with the play. What if she refused to join us? Didn't Ryn say we all had to be together? I took a deep breath and sat there in silence until the car pulled up into the gravel driveway by the Playhouse entrance. We hadn't even come to full stop when I could see one of the girls running towards us. The one with the long braids whose name I never bothered to learn. But apparently, she knew ours.

"Eden! Hurry up! The director just called for a line run-through and then some dance number rehearsals! And Audrey Jane, they need you in the prop area! Opening night is coming up fast!"

Ryn leaned his head out the window.

"Guess I'm off scot-free!"

"Are you working tech crew with Nick?" the girl asked. And then she answered before Ryn could say anything.

"Because if you are, they need all the help they can get. Some sort of animal chewed through the wires and a bunch of stuff needs to be re-connected. Nick is having a fit!"

By now, the car had come to a complete stop and the sheriff turned to face us.

"Well, go on! Looks like all of you have work to do! I'll be in touch. And remember, whatever you do, do not go back to those caves. Understand?"

"Yep," Ryn said as he watched the sheriff back the car out of the drive. The girl with the braids was halfway up to the main door as the three of us started walking. I could tell that Aeden was getting really antsy.

"A line run-through. And then dance numbers. Oh my gosh. We better make sure we're back before the afternoon dress rehearsal tomorrow."

And then, she scampered off as if nothing else mattered but her stupid play. I felt like yanking her by the hair if it weren't so junior high. As things turned out, I didn't have to. Ryn shot after her and grabbed her by the arm.

"Dose of reality, Aeden. Or didn't you think of it? We're going back to that cave tomorrow because that's what we set out to do in the first place. Not get you on Broadway! And I don't know how long it's going to take us tomorrow, so I hope you have an understudy. And a good one!"

Aeden was speechless for a few seconds and then regained her composure.

"I don't have an understudy because I am the understudy!"

"Well you'd better discuss that with the director. And by the way, who exactly is the director? I mean, yeah, I've been busy on the crew with Nick and Phil but I've never seen the director. Just Marcy and Clarisse. What's with that?"

"For your information, the director is Gabe Daniels and he's been out of town for the past few days so Marcy and Clarisse had to take over. I've never worked with him but I did see him when we first got here. Marcy told me that he's under contract with the Playhouse. It's not his investment or anything. He's just paid to work the summer season. And apparently they were really glad to get him. He's been directing plays in Jefferson City and Independence."

"Doesn't that strike you odd, Aeden, that the director goes out of town just days before opening night? Not that I know a hell of a lot about plays, but crap, I wouldn't expect the head coach of the Kansas City Chiefs to take a few days off during the playoffs!"

"So what are you saying? That he might have something to do with Hank Clayton's kidnapping?"

"I'm not saying anything. How well does anyone really know this guy? What the heck. Just add him to the list. As far as I'm concerned, everyone is a suspect. Come on, we'd better get going or we'll be up all night with this rehearsal. You and Ajay need to meet me by the Playhouse truck at 4:00 A.M."

Then he turned to me.

"And Ajay, I mean 4:00 A.M. Don't bother putting on make-up or fussing about your clothes. Just get dressed and get out here."

I opened my mouth to say something but he turned and walked so quickly that by the time words had formed in my mouth, he was already opening the door to the building. Aeden shrugged and gave me a weird look as she darted off in the direction of the stage. Then, she quickly turned and spoke.

"He just doesn't understand show business, Ajay. That's his problem."

Chapter Fifty-one:
Ryn

~

I didn't really think Aeden's director had anything to do with the kidnapping, but heck, I wasn't about to rule out anyone. I had a pretty good idea about the theft, after overhearing that little conversation between Lon and Phil, but were they the kidnappers or did they just need the money?

Aeden had already gone inside by the time I got to the door. I could hear voices coming from the stage but they weren't as loud as the stage crew. Apparently, the wires and sound system were a mess. Terrific. A whole night of re-wiring stuff. Last time I had to do anything like that was when our old cat, Elroyblues, chewed up the speaker wires to Dad's stereo system. I had a feeling this was going to be a whole lot worse. I just hoped my sister would remember to snag a couple of those glass animals. But I wasn't counting on it. Aeden had become such an airhead over her part in the play. But Ajay could get them. Didn't that girl say they needed help with the props?

I immediately turned around and backtracked to the door just as Ajay was walking in.

"Listen, I need you to get some of those glass animals. OK?"

"But I thought Aeden----."

"She won't remember. Trust me. She won't remember. So just get some."

"No problem. Ryn, do you really think it was a squirrel or mice that chewed up the stuff? What if that time loop opened again and it was something else that did the chewing?"

"Then all the more reason for us to get back to the cave and back to the Ice Age to save Hank. Now hurry up!"

Ajay made a face and turned away. Between her and my sister, it was unbearable. At least Linna was normal. Normal and non-existent in 1952. I have a non-existent girlfriend thanks to the time-space continuum. Could the night get any worse? Then, I heard the yelling. Apparently, the wires weren't the only things that got chewed. Part of the roof just collapsed.

"Ryan, there you are!" Nick yelled. "Give Phil a hand clearing the debris. It's way off –stage but we've got to deal with it right now. Phil will have to get to the lumberyard first thing in the morning to get plywood and shingles. It was just a matter of time. I knew the damn roof needed to be replaced."

"Yeah," Phil said as he dragged a barrel over to the corner where the wood had fallen. "I always enjoy a good reason to get up at the crack of dawn."

I gave Phil a cold stare and spoke slowly.

"Too bad someone stole the money or maybe this place would have had a roof by now."

"What good's a new roof if the highway goes through it? We're all sitting ducks just waiting for that commission to make its decision. Come on, give me a hand with this junk."

As we lifted pieces of broken wood into the barrel, I began to think about the commission and Hank's role on it. His was the deciding vote according to Owen. And that's the second I knew I could figure out this whole thing.

"Be back in a second, Phil. I need to talk to a girl."

"Right this minute?"

But I never answered him. I was already backstage looking for the prop room.

Chapter Fifty-two:
Ajay

Ryn was in my face before I even knew what was going on so I jumped at him.

"I told you already I'd get those glass animals. You didn't have to charge in here like a maniac."

"Shh! It's not about the animals. I may know who's responsible for kidnapping your great-grandfather. Listen carefully. Whoever it was, they didn't want him to vote on the highway decision. And he didn't. So whatever decision got made in 1952, it's the one that exists today. Today in our time. I can't believe I didn't think of this before. Ajay—where the hell is highway 125?"

"My God, Ryn. It runs north of the city and parallels the college campus. That means..."

"Yeah, I know. Now here's the thing. Who were the members of that 1952 commission? Do you know their names?"

"Are you insane? How on earth would I know something like that? I don't even remember the names of the first ten presidents of the United States. Well, maybe Washington, Jefferson and

Adams. But I don't even know the order. And were there two Adamses?"

"Oh, geez, Ajay, just try to think."

"You're nuts, Ryn. No one knows that stuff. That's why we have computers. And smartphones. All the history and news in an instant. Why torture our brains?"

"What did you just say?"

"I said, 'why torture our brains.'"

"No, the other thing. The news. It would be in the news. In a newspaper. A newspaper in 1952. This highway vote is a big deal. It's got to be in one of the local newspapers. And they've got to list the members of the commission. Well, don't just stand there, help me find a newspaper!"

Ryn was like a madman. And he was beginning to freak me out.

"Look. I'm just going over to the boxes where the glass animals are. Before I forget and it's too late. Maybe there's an old newspaper in the kitchen."

"Right. I'll check the kitchen."

Ryn left in more of a hurry than when he first came in. But I knew if I didn't grab one or two of those glass figurines, we wouldn't have them. So, I opened the box and started to un-wrap them. Newspaper! They were wrapped in newspaper! I almost raced after Ryn, but decided to look at the articles first. Sports, home and garden, obituaries, and then, a small article that was cut off on the bottom. But the names were there. All four of them. And Hank Clayton was going to be number five.

I stuffed the article in my pocket and headed to the kitchen, making sure that I put everything back the way it was, except for the small swan and deer that I hid. Ryn was leafing through every old paper and magazine in sight and jumped as soon as he heard my voice.

"Eugene Brickson, Lloyd Meldridge, Raymond Finley, and Arthur Gaines."

"What?"

"The names, Ryn. I found the names. They used newspapers to pack those glass animals. Here – see for yourself. And what a pain in the neck. Leftover newspapers with recipes cut out, coupons cut out and all sorts of stuff cut out. You owe me for this!"

Ryn took the yellowed piece of paper and read the story. It was written months ago. And it made no mention of Hank Clayton, only that a fifth appointee would be nominated. But Ryn had the names. I just didn't see how he could figure out the rest. But before I could ask him, the girl with the braids walked in and plopped herself in the nearest chair.

"I'm pooped. They gave us a ten minute break. Did you hear about the roof? Guess they'll be hammering and banging all morning. My head already hurts."

"Well, I'd better get going," Ryn announced as he left the room. "Nick and Phil will be looking for me. By the way, Audrey Jane, I wanted three apple muffins, not four. Be sure to let my sister know."

"Apple muffins?" the girl asked. "Did someone bake muffins?"

"I'm not sure. Um...maybe."

Three apple muffins, not four. Three ap...oh hell. Apple muffins. A.M. He wants us to meet him at 3:00 A.M. and not 4:00. I'll have bags under my eyes. And no make-up.

The girl with the braids stood up and yawned.

"Well, I don't have time to find out. I'd better get back to the stage before something else breaks down or falls apart. Honestly, maybe the best thing would be for this place to close and have a highway run through it."

"You don't really mean that, do you?"

"No, of course not. But let me tell you, there are lots of people in this area who do. Like those Stocktons from the car dealership. Clarisse's brother told her that the Stocktons plan on building fast food restaurants once the highway goes through. Can you imagine? Fast food? It sounds awful."

I wanted to tell her that I'd throw myself over a bridge for a Big Mac or a Whopper but she wouldn't get it. Instead, I tried to find out more about the highway.

"Do you think the Stocktons would go so far as to kidnap someone to get their way?"

"I don't know about that...but I can tell you one thing. When the Stocktons want something, nothing gets in their way."

She tossed one of her braids behind her neck and left the kitchen before I could say anything else. Everyone in the cast was edgy and the braid girl was no exception. With all the interruptions, I knew they needed more rehearsal time. But as things turned out, they weren't going to get it. The lights in the kitchen began to flicker and I heard someone yell, "Damn it! More wires got chewed up!"

Chapter Fifty-three:
Ryn

I figured Ajay was bright enough to get the message. We had to be in the truck and on our way to the caves by 3:00 A.M. Any later and the truck would be heading to the lumberyard with Phil. I was pissed that he blew off my comment about the roof; especially since I figured he and his Dad were the ones who stole the repair money to begin with. To "grease someone's palms." Isn't that what they said? For all I know, they could have arranged for the kidnapping themselves. So what was I waiting for? Phil was just a few feet away, trying to piece together some wire. *It's now or never*. As I walked towards him, he immediately looked up.

"About time you got back, Ryan. The director just sent the cast home for the night. Called an early rehearsal as soon as we can fix the wiring and shore up the roof."

"Yeah, about the wiring...isn't it a little too coincidental that things are going to hell around here? It's as if someone wants the place to close. So, let me ask you something. Why did you steal the $5,000 from the roof money?"

"What? You're accusing me of taking that money? Where did you get a cockamamie idea like that?"

I took a step back just in case the guy felt like slugging me. Then, I continued.

"I don't make it a point to listen in on other peoples' conversations, but the one between you and your dad the other day was loud enough for everyone to hear. Too bad I was the only one standing there. So don't lie. I heard both of you. You paid someone the money to buy you some influence about the highway vote so the lumberyard wouldn't go out of business. And don't give me that crap about the end justifying the means."

Phil motioned for me to have a seat on one of the stools. He cleared his throat and spoke softly.

"You've got it wrong. About stealing the money from Nick's office. I'd never do a thing like that and neither would my Dad."

"Go on."

"My father emptied his entire savings to make that pay-off. If my mother ever found out, it would kill her. That savings was the only security they had. But if the lumberyard folded, they'd have nothing. So, yeah. You heard right. You just jumped to the wrong conclusion."

I stared at Phil and felt like a louse. So much for my detective skills. I'll cross that career off my list, too.

"I don't know what to say, Phil. I'm sorry. It's just that—."

"Don't worry about it. Just give me a hand with this wiring."

I reached over for some wire nuts and began to piece a few strands of metal together when I realized that I hadn't asked him who they paid off. But it was too late. Nick had walked backstage, shoved a piece of notebook paper at us and spoke before I could say anything.

"Get a load of this. I found it on the seat of the truck. I have no idea how long it's been there. I left my cigarettes and lighter on the dash, so I went back to get them before you took off tomorrow. Looks like one of those ransom notes from an old 1930's movie. Someone took the time to paste those newspaper letters. At first I thought it might be some sort of corny joke, but now I'm not so sure. Read it."

"You'll get your money back. Call off the sheriff."

"So," Nick continued. "What do you think?"

It was obvious that someone must have gone to a lot of trouble to write that note because the letters were small and cutting them out must have been a real pain in the butt. So I figured it had to be someone from the Playhouse whose handwriting would be recognized. And someone who handles props. It didn't take a genius for that one. Ajay had just told me that the glass animals were wrapped in newspapers that had lots of articles cut-up. I didn't need the sheriff to make another trip out here. They'd be all over the truck and I needed it the next morning.

"I wouldn't do anything if I were you, Nick." I said. "Give it some time and wait for whoever took the money to return it. If you don't get it back in a week, then call the sheriff. Just tell him you didn't want to risk losing the five grand for good or you would have called him sooner."

Phil nodded in agreement.

"The kid's right. I'd give it at least a day or two."

Nick shrugged and started to walk out.

"Guess I'll put this in the safe. It's the only evidence we have."

Phil laughed.

"It's the only thing we have. If all else fails, we can always use it as a prop if we decide to produce a mystery next season."

Chapter Fifty-four:
Clarisse

The battered 1946 Chevy squealed as Andy Pendleton jammed on the brakes. He pulled it off to the side of the Playhouse driveway and walked inside. He could hear people talking on stage and thought it was a full rehearsal, considering that the lights were only lit in certain areas. He waited until someone was nearby and then spoke.

"I don't want to interrupt the rehearsal, but I'm looking for my sister Clarisse."

"You're not interrupting much of anything," the guy wearing a tan shirt and jeans replied. "The lights aren't working right, the roof sort of fell in near the prop area and the cast is about ready to call it a night."

"Do you know who Clarisse is? Can you get her for me?"

"Sure, everyone knows her. Hold on. I'll send her over."

The guy disappeared into the darkness, leaving Andy to look around. Even with the dim lighting he could see that the Playhouse was in need of repairs. And not just small ones. From the splintery chairs to the peeling paint on the walls, it was clear that only a major renovation would save the place. And who wanted to pour money into the Mark Twain Playhouse if the highway decision was in favor of another plan? Andy took out a handkerchief and started to wipe his nose just as Clarisse approached.

"Andy, what are you doing here? What's wrong?"

"Is there a private place where we can talk? Where no one can hear us?"

"Not really. The cast and crew are everywhere."

"I really need to talk to you. Let's just go back to my truck. Guess it's the only safe place."

Clarisse nodded and followed her brother outside.

"Sounds ominous," she said as she climbed into the cab.

"Nothing's wrong. I just wanted to apologize and I didn't want anyone to hear."

"Apologize? For what?"

"For putting you in that position with the gun. Randy Tinger paid me over a hundred dollars to hold on to that gun for him until he needed it. And I couldn't leave it around the house. Not with kids and all."

"I understand. But you don't think that gun was used in any...um..." Then Clarisse grabbed her brother's arm."Oh my gosh ---that gun wasn't used to kidnap Hank Clayton, was it?"

"I don't know. I honestly don't know. Randy got the gun from a guy over in Rolla. I was just supposed to hold on to it for a few days and I did. Or I should say, you did. Randy told me he needed it for some big deal with his brother-in-law Darnell. Sounded more like a 'for show' kind of thing than an actual crime. Heck, the bullets weren't even in the barrel. Remember? I gave them to you in an envelope."

"I know. I put them in the glove compart-ment of the Playhouse truck, where no one bothers to look. And I stashed the gun under the front seat. Normally Nick keeps a silly cap gun there. I managed to swap things back just in time so I could return the .38 to you. But the bullets were gone."

"I'm really sorry, Clarisse. Really. I never should have put you in this position. But I needed the money bad. Things have not been going well on the farm."

"But bad enough to get involved with that slimy Randy? What else did he tell you?"

"Nothing much but he seemed to think that he and his brother-in-law were about to land on a boatload of money."

"Do you remember exactly what he said?"

"Yeah. Because it sounded like something out of an old movie. *Darnell found us some big shot with money up the wazoo. We just need to do him a favor.*"

"Andy, that favor might have been to kidnap Hank Clayton. You've got to tell the sheriff. It can't wait. Promise me you'll tell him."

Before Andy could give her his answer, someone started to pound on the window.

"Clarisse! There you are!"

Marcy looked distraught and exhausted.

"I didn't mean to cut your visit short but the director needs to see us now. He's really worried about opening night and so am I."

Clarisse leaned over and gave her brother a hug before getting out of the truck. As her face neared his ear, she whispered two words.

"Call him."

Chapter Fifty-five:
Aeden

"**P**sst! Aeden! Wake-up! Your brother is driving me nuts!"

Ajay was standing over my cot and I had no idea what time it was.

"Oh my God. Is it 4:00 A.M.? Are we late?"

"No, it's just a little after midnight. The entire crew had to stay and help with clean-up. At least you got to sleep. And your brother wants us out by the truck at three, not four."

"Are you kidding me?"

"He's a lunatic! He also expected me to know who was on the Missouri Highway Commission in 1952!"

"Huh?"

"Yeah, he thinks he can figure out who the kidnapper was, or is. Anyway, we've got to get to the truck early. Ryn probably found out that someone else will be using it. So we need to beat them to it."

"Then we'd better get back here early, too. The director called a morning rehearsal as soon as the crew finishes with the wiring and repairs. Oh no! Oh no! My brother's going to kill me! I forgot those glass animals."

"He thought you would. I've got them. I took two of them. They're wrapped up in an old shirt in a brown bag that I found in the kitchen."

"What about the flashlight and batteries?"

"Ryn already put them in the back of the truck. I kept watch when everyone left the Playhouse tonight."

Ajay threw off her jeans and climbed into the cot next to mine.

"I'm exhausted Aeden. Totally. My God. I'm too tired to wash my face. Every one of my pores is going to clog up. I can't wait till this is over with. So what happens now? We find my great-grandfather and get him to 1952 and then we get back to our own time?"

The girl still didn't get it. It wasn't a freaking plane schedule. Still, it was an oscillating time loop and I was counting on it, too. Just for a few performances. Enough to get me noticed. My God, I was just as bad as she was. Maybe worse because I knew better. Still, I figured we'd either find Hank Clayton alive and we'd all get back here in time for opening night or...we'd just be spectators in a history that was long gone, along with her great- grandfather.

"It's unpredictable, Ajay, but I know that time seems to have its own weird structure and it doesn't like things to be out of place. We'll get back here all right. We have to!"

"But what if something goes really wrong and my great- grandfather gets pushed forward into the 21st century? Then what?"

"I don't know. I'm not Einstein or Stephen Hawking and I can't stop and worry about it. I've got to concentrate on my lines and my musical numbers."

"You've gotten so selfish Aeden."

"I'm not selfish. You and Ryn don't understand. You don't get a lead role in Summer Theater just like that."

Ajay adjusted her pillow and sighed.

"Promise me, Aeden, that you won't decide to ditch us at the last minute."

"No one's getting ditched. Now get to sleep. We only have about 3 hours."

I closed my eyes and listened to Ajay toss around on the narrow cot. No one else in the cabin had heard us. They were all asleep. Asleep and unaware that in the next 24 hours, everything would change.

Chapter Fifty-six:
Ryn

Good thing there was still some moonlight or it would have been impossible to see the truck. And I wasn't about to turn on the flashlight. Aeden and Ajay were already standing in the driveway. A first. Aeden was on time for something. I motioned with my finger to the lips for them to keep quiet. Then I whispered as soon as I got closer.

"I grabbed the keys last night when everyone left the Playhouse. But we can't start the truck in the driveway or someone will hear us. I'll step on the clutch, put it in neutral and you two can give it a push from the back. It should roll down the drive. Then, I'll turn on the lights and start it."

Ajay gave me a shove.

"Why do I have to push it? Can't you do that?"

"Look, if I thought for the smallest instant, that you or my sister could drive a stick shift, I'd let you. But we've already seen how good that turned out for you before. So just let me do it and quit complaining. We haven't got all night."

The girls didn't say another word and walked to the back of the truck. I put the flashlight on the front seat next to the glass animals that Ajay handed me. Then, I got inside. This was worse than my road test. If someone caught me, I'd never be able to explain it. I could feel those small sticky beads of sweat on my eyebrow as I maneuvered the steering wheel. It was heavy and tough to begin with, not an automatic, and without the engine on, it felt like steering an anvil.

I turned on the headlights once I was sure we were in the road. Ajay and Aeden crammed into the front seat and I turned the key.

"Just don't break those glass things, Aeden," I said as we got further down the road. "And whatever you two do, don't turn on the flashlight. We need to conserve the batteries."

Ajay took offense as usual.

"We're not stupid, Ryn."

"Didn't say you were."

My sister started making those idiotic clicking noises with her tongue and the roof of her mouth. She does that when she's pissed or nervous. And I knew she wasn't nervous.

"How much longer till we get there?"

"My God, Aeden. It's like you're five years old. We'll be there in a few minutes. We just got on the main road, and then I have to turn off and go down that narrow road to the caves. I'll try to park this thing as close to that hole-in-the-ground opening as I can."

"It's creepy out here on the road at night," Ajay said as she turned and looked behind us. "No one else is around."

"That's a good thing. We don't want anyone around. We can't afford to be followed. Now as soon as we get there, I'll grab the flashlight. Aeden, just hold on to those glass animals, OK?"

"Uh- huh."

I kept talking.

"Ajay, you'll need to hold the flashlight as I go down the hole first. Then, toss it to me and I'll hold it up against the wall for both of you to see when you climb in. Got it?"

It should have been an easy process. But no. Ajay didn't want to be last and neither did Aeden. We finally settled on Aeden going first, then Ajay and then me. No wonder girls have their own sports' teams! No one else would put up with them!

The girls managed to lower themselves into the hole without too much complaining. Either that or I had gotten so used to their whining that it just became background noise, like static. I took a breath and looked back at the truck. It was plenty visible against the rock wall. All I could do was cross my fingers that no one would find it before we got back.

The ground in that part of the cave was level and the air was cold, even with a sweatshirt on. I bounced the flashlight beam across the walls as we headed to the spot where we had seen the shirt sleeve melded into the rock.

The only sounds were the soft crunching of our shoes and our breathing. I never thought breathing would be so loud. Hell, our furnace wasn't even as loud. But no one spoke. Not even a complaint, and when Aeden finally said something, it was barely audible.

Chapter Fifty-seven:
Ajay

It sounded like a raspy, squeaky noise. Like the kind hamsters make in their cages. I never expected it to be coming from Aeden. Even with the indirect light from the beam, I could see her mouthing something.

"Bu..Bu...bugs..."

And then I saw for myself. The entire wall where Aeden had placed her hand was covered with tiny insects. Pill bugs. Hundreds of them. And some of them had fallen from crevices above onto our heads. I went berserk.

"Get them off me! Get them off me!"

Ryn slapped the upside of my head as if it was the rear of a horse and he wanted to get it going.

"It's just little harmless bugs. Pill bugs. Roly polys. You don't freak out when you see them in the corner of your basement, do you?"

Then Aeden started to scream.

"We have these in our basement? I'm never going home!"

"Stop it, both of you. Just shake yourselves off and keep going. This is ridiculous."

We continued in single file, watching the beam as Ryn methodically waved it on each wall. Then, he held it steady and spoke.

"Over there! Take a look! I can see the shirt sleeve from here!"

My hands began to sweat as we got closer. Images of giant mammals suddenly came to mind and I realized just how terrible this was going to be.

"We didn't bring any weapons, did we? I mean, we should have. We should have thought of it."

Just then, Ryn took something from his back pocket and held it out for us to see.

"It's just that old cowboy cap gun from the truck, but it has caps and makes a lot of noise. At least it might frighten something. Now come on."

Next thing I knew, Ryn was figuring out where to place the small glass swan.

"Someone's got to hold it. There's no place to put it. So, here's the deal. Aeden, you hold the swan. Ajay, you need to light a match and make sure it's next to the glass. I'll be right behind with the flashlight. On 'GO' we all do this. And we've got to get it right. Whatever you do, don't move from where you're standing."

I couldn't budge if I wanted to. If I made a move, the fire from the match would have burnt my fingers. That's how badly I was shaking. I just stared at the flame, willing it to stay still.

Everything around me flickered and shook. It was like watching strobe lights without the music. I expected something worse. Like a blinding flash or rocks crashing everywhere. But none of that happened. Instead, the flashlight beam got dimmer, the light from the match went out and the cave suddenly felt wet and moist. I had to say something.

"Maybe we should try this again. Maybe it will work next time."

Then I heard Aeden's voice.

"Don't move, Ajay. It already did."

Chapter Fifty-eight:
Hank Clayton

*H*ank Clayton lost his footing and slipped quickly and noiselessly into the crevice just as the gunshot ripped through the cave and shook the rock walls. Small pieces of stalactites cracked and fell, making the ground appear as if it had been hit by a hailstorm. For an instant, Hank couldn't hear anything. The pressure in his ears was so intense that all he could do was force himself to swallow.

That guy thinks I'm dead. No sense changing his opinion.

The bottom of his palms were scraped, as well as his knees, but other than that, Hank was all right. Part of his shirt was ripped off but the rest of his clothing remained intact. He forced himself to stay face down in the dirt until he was certain that Darnell Legrun had walked off. Then, he stood up and lifted his arms high enough to feel the top ledge of the crevice.

Talk about dumb luck. If this hole wasn't here, that bullet would've gone through my head. I'll need to wait it out until I hear the sound of an engine starting and tires rolling on gravel. When that guy's out of here, I'll start for the road and try to hitch a ride.

Hank moved his hands slowly across the top of the drop-off and that's when he felt the gun. Darnell never bothered to pick it up. The barrel was still warm. Jumping high enough to place his arms on top of the hole, Hank hoisted himself up, using the small rock cut-offs to support his weight. Panting with exhaustion, he reached for the gun and held it to his chest before tucking it into the back of his waistband.

Place is as dark as night. It must be later than I thought. And I'm hearing water. Some sort of stream. Didn't know these caves had creeks running through them.

With a steady motion, Hank grabbed the lighter from his shirt and flicked it once. He could see the outline of the cave and a winding bend of fast moving water. He tightened his grip on the lighter.

If I follow the stream, it's bound to take me to the entrance or at least the source. Good thing I just re-filled this baby with lighter fluid.

It was a slow, uneventful trek out of the cave and Hank could make out the night sky in the distance. He smiled for an instant as he remembered pointing out the constellations to his dad when they'd go camping. He planned to do the same thing with his own kids when they got older.

Ursa major...ursa minor...forming the Big Dipper

And then Hank seemed to choke on his own breath momentarily.

The stars are here. It's the night sky. But something's wrong. These constellations should be in a different position in the sky. It's summer. Summer of 1952, but not according to what I'm looking at.

Before he could gather his thoughts coherently, a wailing, shrieking noise just a few yards from where he was standing, gave him a shudder that seemed to drop his body temperature by degrees.

Something just made a kill. Coyotes maybe. But no coyote ever made that sound. Maybe it's not such a great idea getting to the road at night. I'm waiting it out in the cave. Daybreak will come soon enough.

Hank turned and headed back to the cave. He figured by morning there would be lots of cars and people out looking for him. He could survive one uncomfortable night. Not a bad price to pay for narrowly escaping death.

Then, he heard the noises again. Louder wailing. They were getting closer.

Chapter Fifty-nine: *Clarisse*

Clarisse threw off the itchy blue blanket that was standard issue for cast and crew and decided instead to sleep in her sweatshirt and jeans. By now, everyone in the cabin was asleep except her. The meeting with the director was short and to the point – no one was ready for opening night but they had no choice.

The technical difficulties would be resolved in time, but that didn't mean something else wasn't about to go wrong. And then there was the matter of the cast. That new girl was pretty good, but "so flaky" according to Marcy.

"I have a bad feeling about this, Clarisse," Marcy said shortly after their meeting with Gabe. "I just keep thinking that Eden girl is going to mess up somehow."

"Have you talked to her about it?"

"No, I didn't want to unnerve her, especially the day before we open."

"Do we have any other options?"

"If you mean, is there anyone else to play that part, just in case, then the answer is no. You know, Clarisse, maybe this is just a summer theater for most folks, but for me it's the only opportunity I'll have to get a break and maybe a job off-Broadway or something like that. Did you know that Gabe drove all the way to St. Louis to be sure that an agent would be here tomorrow to see the performance? To see me?"

"No, I didn't know that. I wondered why he was out of town at such a crucial time. But, yeah, I understand how important this is to you. And how important it is for the Playhouse to stay open. At any cost. By the way, I had an interesting conversation the other day with my brother, who picks up all the gossip from the lumberyard. He told me that one of the commission members was open to being swayed."

"Swayed how?"

"How do you think, Marcy? With money. A pay-off. And it almost happened."

"Clarisse, what are you talking about?"

"I did something awful. Only, in the end, I really didn't. I found out that Councilman Barkley's uncle, Arthur Gaines, was not above taking bribes. So...I kind of took the money that Nick had in the safe to give to Mr. Gaines in order to buy his vote. It would have saved all of us. All of our jobs. Only, in the end, I couldn't do it. So, I just got back from returning that money. Nick will find it tomorrow. Please don't tell! Please don't say a word to anyone!"

"Holy Cow, Clarisse! I can't believe you did something like that!"

"I was only trying to help and I didn't know what else to do."

"Guess there's really no harm done. But we did lose a full rehearsal!"

"I know. I feel like such a fool."

"A fool with good intentions. Anyway, try to get some sleep. What's done is done."

"So you're really worried about that Eden girl?"

"Worried enough."

Clarisse shut her eyes and started to doze off, but it was a light sleep. Every noise from the crickets outside the cabin to the crunching of footsteps from people on their way to the latrine woke her up. She was certain that two of the girls in her own bunk decided to use the facilities in the middle of the night. She heard the slight creak from the screen door as the girls slipped out.

It was too dark to tell which ones they were, and by the time Clarisse found out, it was already past dawn.

Chapter Sixty:
Aeden

I was still holding the tiny glass swan. My fingers hadn't moved from their original position. If it weren't for the fact that the temperature had dropped and a putrid fecal stench filed the air, I would have sworn nothing had happened.

"Hear that?" Ryn said as he stepped towards Ajay and me. "It's the sound of water rushing. Water in the cave. We've tripped back. No headaches. No nausea. Nothing. Just like that. We've tripped back. Now we just need to find Hank Clayton."

Ajay opened her mouth and started to yell for him when my brother slammed his palm over it.

"Shh! What are you thinking? You could be inviting every carnivorous creature around. We've got to do this thing quickly and quietly."

Then, he flicked on the flashlight and held it up. The light was faint, but visible enough for us to see the rock walls, and the fast moving stream to our right. The rock formations seemed larger somehow, clumsier, as if time hadn't yet sculpted them out.

"Look, we can't afford to wear down the batteries so we'll need to get a look at our bearings and then try to rely on using the matches instead. You and Ajay OK with that?"

Before I could reply, Ajay made herself clear. "Whatever."

Then Ryn continued whispering.

"We were standing right in the spot where the shirt sleeve was, so start looking around and stay together. And take short steps. This place is full of holes and crevices."

The glow from the match light was smaller and more intense than the flashlight. I kept looking down but all I could see were Ajay and Ryn's sneakers.

"Watch out, Ajay! You nearly got us killed. You were heading straight for that hole!"

Even when he spoke softly, my brother's voice could be intimidating. And then there was Ajay. She wasn't about to let anyone have the last word.

"Well, what do you expect? I could barely see."

I edged slowly to the opening and tried to look down.

"Use the flashlight for a second, Ryn. I mean, this hole is awfully close to where that sleeve was."

And sure enough, I was right. In the dim light

we could see the fragments of the checkered red and white shirt lying at the bottom of the fissure. It was eerie. Even though it was just a piece of cloth, it felt as if we had found the remains of some hapless creature. I gasped and so did Ajay. Only my brother appeared to be nonchalant.

"Well, he's here all right. He must have climbed out. By now he could be anywhere in this cave...or worse yet, outside."

"My God, Ryn," I said. "He has no idea what he's about to face."

Then we heard that horrid wailing sound of a fresh kill. It was coming from the cave's entrance.

"He does by now, Aeden. Hurry up, both of you. Let's hope the batteries hold out. The sound must be coming from outside. That means the entrance isn't too far off."

Our feet seemed to move automatically as we got closer to the yipping noise. Then Ajay grabbed my brother from the shoulder and spoke.

"What's our plan now? What are we going to do?"

I knew better than to ask "Mr.-Last-Minute-Work-From-The-Seat-Of-Your-Pants" something like that, so it was no surprise when he answered.

"Whatever we have to."

Chapter Sixty-one:
Councilman Barkley

Bob Barkley turned his head away from the door and continued talking on the phone.

"That moronic brother-in-law of yours should have been back by now. What do you mean you haven't heard from him? Have you tried looking?"

Randy Tinger stuttered and stammered as he responded.

"I was supposed to …I mean…things kinda changed at the last minute."

Then he told the councilman everything about the incident and held his breath as Bob Barkley exploded.

"This was supposed to be a simple matter. And now what? Is it going to turn into a murder? Is that what I'm about to hear?"

"I don't know, sir. Honest, I don't. We just couldn't leave that Hank guy to identify us."

"Well, you'd better keep that stupid yap of yours shut, you hear? Because I'm not going down for murder, understand?"

"Yes, yes I do."

Then, Bob Barkley slammed the phone into the receiver before picking it up again to make one more call. One that Noreen Brown overheard as she walked back to the file cabinets.

"Get me Ed Stockton on the phone now!" he roared. Then, he cleared his throat and continued.

"We got a problem, Ed. Those two imbeciles messed things up with our staged little kidnapping and now I think the one guy may actually kill Hank Clayton if he hasn't done so already."

"What? What are you saying? You and I agreed that we were just going to get Hank out of the way until after that vote. And your Uncle Arthur was going to pull some strings on the board. Darn it all. I needed that highway to cut off the Playhouse and the Percy Lumberyard so I could develop that strip mall. But murder? I never agreed to murder! Now what do we do?"

Bob Barkley lowered his voice but it was still audible on the other side of the door.

"We keep our yaps shut, that's what. I have an election coming up and the last I knew, felons can't run for office. Don't do another thing. The hell with your strip mall. If we try anything else, we'd just be calling attention to ourselves. Stay still. Got it?"

Noreen leaned in closer, pretending to look at an open file on the top of the drawer. But she took the pencil out from behind her ear and used the shorthand she learned in her high school business class to write down every single word of that conversation. Then, she left the office telling the workers she needed a cup of coffee. But when she entered the café across the street, she went straight to the pay phones and dialed the sheriff.

Chapter Sixty-two: Hank Clayton

Hank Clayton starred into the darkness from the mouth of the cave. The shrieking, yelping sounds had stopped suddenly, if as the celebration over a fresh kill had ended. He took a breath and stepped outside. Even in the moonlight, everything looked wrong. The outline of the hills wasn't right and the tall, angular trees were nowhere in sight. Instead, shorter, bushier versions crowded the entrance.

No driveway. There should be a well-worn driveway from years of cars flattening the dirt ground.

He paused to turn around and go back into the cave when he heard the unmistakable noise of something approaching from behind.

It's moving towards me. A bear maybe? A coyote?

Hank took a quick breath and darted into the first clump of trees he could make out in the dim light. The sharp, earthy smell filled his nostrils as he held still and waited for whatever was in the cave to step out. This wasn't a time for indecision. He'd have to use that gun if he expected to survive.

Chapter Sixty-three:
Ryn

I never liked playing "Hide and Seek" as a kid. And it didn't matter which role I had. They both stunk. So where was Hank Clayton hiding? If we didn't find him and warn him about where he was, it might be too late. If we all stayed together, we stood some sort of a chance to make it out of here without being the appetizer, lunch and dinner for a giant sloth or a saber-toothed tiger.

Ajay and Aeden didn't say a word as we approached the front of the cave. Outside, the war chant that signaled "kill and eat time" had ended.

Aeden nudged me.

"It stopped. The noises stopped. You don't suppose that they ate...."

"I don't know what to think."

"My God!" Ajay gasped.

"Look," I whispered. "We don't know anything so stop getting hysterical."

Ajay mumbled something but I couldn't hear the first part. Only a request to turn on the flashlight.

"No way! You know we can't take a chance on having whatever's out there seeing us. Just try to look around the shadows and stay close to the cave entrance."

I swear she made a spitting sound, but then again, it could just have been my imagination. We moved out slowly, just inches from each other. And that's the second that one of the girls stumbled and I heard a clear, rustling noise from the bushes and trees a few yards from us.

Chapter Sixty-four:
Hank Clayton

Hank Clayton heard the noise from the front of the cave and could see the outline of a creature ambling towards him. It bent down for a second but came up and moved slowly. Taller than anything he would have expected. Only an elk would have that height, or maybe a moose, but not in Missouri.

He aimed the gun straight at the neck, but then he realized that there was more than one. A gunshot might anger the others. Then again, he had enough target practice to fire rapid rounds if he needed to. The combination of darkness and the first mist of morning made it impossible to discern what kind of creature was stepping out of the cave. Hank kept his hand steady and stood absolutely still.

Then, from behind, in a smaller clump of bushes, a fat, squat peccary started to root through the grass, causing Hank to turn away from the cave for an instant. By now, the faintest grey light illuminated the horizon and the stars disappeared from the night sky.

Javelina! What the heck is a javelina doing in Missouri? I thought those things were in the southwest for crying out loud!

By the time Hank turned to face the cave, the animal that stood at least five or six feet tall had left its lair. Slowly, without loosening his grip, Hank moved the gun until it was barrel down, resting next to his thigh.

In the early light, Hank could see a large ridge above the cave's entrance. Ground plants and dense brush surrounded the area.

This is all wrong. All wrong. I must have gotten hit in the head or shot. None of this can be real. Still, I'm not letting go of the damn gun. And I mean it; I'll shoot the first thing that comes at me.

Chapter Sixty-five:
Ajay

It was getting light but there was no sign of my great-grandfather. I figured his clothing would have to show up against the trees and rock but I didn't see anything other than the thick bushes. Aeden and Ryn motioned for me to sidestep the cave entrance and walk along the rock wall. I kept my voice low as I got closer to them.

"Don't tell me otherwise. That wailing sound. And the yelps. Something killed my great-grandfather. I know it. I can smell death in the air."

Ryn snapped back.

"The only thing you smell in the air is the same putrid stink of damp dirt and musk. Same as before. Stop being so dramatic. Save that for my sister."

I couldn't get one syllable out when Aeden opened her mouth.

"I'll never be dramatic again, Ryn. You've ruined that for me."

"Oh for the life of me! Cut it out Aeden! You can win an Oscar when we get back to Portland! And same goes for you, Ajay! I've about had enough! Hank Clayton's no fool, he's probably hiding in one of these clusters of trees. He'll make a move and we'll see him."

I wanted to ask why we couldn't make the move first, but I already knew the answer. We'd be leaving ourselves vulnerable to any number of predators in the area. So I inched closer to Ryn and Aeden, leaning against the rock wall. Above me, the roof from the overhang started to drip and I wiped my forehead.

"Just moisture from the ground," Ryn said. "Step out in front."

Those were the last words I heard or recognized. The sound shattered the air and stung every part of me. A blast? A cannon? And then, the thud. Flat. Loud. Solid. I felt the weight of something knocking me over and when I reached to grab it, all I could feel was thick, dense fur.

Chapter Sixty-six:
Hank Clayton

Something about the roof ledge above the cave bothered Hank. It seemed the perfect perch for any large animal to survey the surrounding area. And then, he saw a slight movement. Off to the side. Something crawling slowly. Carefully. It was a struggle to see anything behind the dense foliage but whatever it was, it was moving.

Maybe that animal already jumped down and is eyeballing me.

Hank pointed the gun towards the movement.

I've got you now, buddy. Make one move and you're history.

In a flash, Hank caught a quick movement above the ledge. It was full daylight now and as he stepped out into the clearing, what he saw convinced him that indeed, he had been shot in the head.

The tiger's face was small and out of proportion in comparison to the large fangs that curved on either side of its jaw. And before Hank could even see the color of its fur, it jumped directly above whatever was standing against the rock wall.

I'll take my chances with the smaller beasts, but not you, buddy.

And then, without wasting a moment of thought, Hank aimed the barrel straight between the fangs and pulled the trigger. A clear shot. Right through the head. In mid jump, the tiger went rigid and fell, knocking something onto the ground.

Hank could feel his hand trembling, still clutching the gun.

Lawdy, lawdy, Miss Clawdy. This better be over with damn soon.

Chapter Sixty-seven:
Ryn

It happened so fast that I didn't have time to process it. Better that way. No lasting images to tell a shrink about. Just the aftermath and I'd better not get any freaking nightmares over it.

One minute I'm telling Ajay to step out from under the dripping rock and the next thing I know, we're inches from being blasted in the head with a gun. But the guy's aim was good. Better than good. It was only one shot and suddenly this giant saber-tooth tiger comes barreling over the ledge knocking Ajay to the ground with its hind legs. If she had stepped out further, she would have been crushed from the weight.

I looked down and could see her reaching out with a hand over the cat's rump. Aeden was pressed against the rock wall, too numb to move. I waved her over.

"It's OK. The thing's dead and Ajay is just stunned, that's all."

"That's all? Isn't that enough?"

Then, a thought occurred to me. It had to be Hank Clayton and he was still holding a gun. Animals or not, I took my chances and shouted.

"Don't shoot! There's three of us! Don't shoot!"

A few yards away, I heard his response.

"Who are you? And where are we?"

"We're with the Mark Twain Playhouse and we're in Missouri."

"This is one hell of a play, kid. Stay right where you are."

Chapter Sixty-eight:
Marcy Meadows

Marcy looked up from her seat at the small table next to Nick's desk in the theater office. Her eyes were swollen from crying and her nose was running.

"We'll just have to refund the tickets, Nick. I can't believe they walked out on us."

"Drove out, you mean. Anyway, we can always open in the next couple of weeks once we find a replacement for that Eden girl."

"But we will have lost most of the season. And the agents. This is a disaster. What did that note say again?"

"It wasn't specific. Ryan must have written it late last night and left it on my desk. He apologized and said that he and the girls had to get back to Portland. Never meant to mess us up. But stealing our truck? Don't worry. The sheriff will find them."

Just then, they heard the sound of gravel crunching on the driveway. Marcy stood up, looked out the window and saw Noreen Brown stepping out of a small sedan.

"It's not the truck, Nick. Someone's here to see me, I think. I'll be right back."

The woman brushed some strands of hair from her face and spoke before Marcy could even say "hello."

"Marcy, I'm so sorry about the way I spoke to you the other day. I would have been fired if my boss caught me having a personal phone call. I guess it really doesn't matter anymore. Some job I had, working for that scoundrel and cheat. By now, I hope the sheriff has arrested him and his partners for the kidnapping of Hank Clayton. And who knows, it might even be murder. A bunch of them were in cahoots, beginning with Councilman Barkley."

"Oh my gosh. That's awful. What are you going to do now?"

"I'm not sure. I certainly don't or won't have a job in his campaign office."

"You can always go back to your old one. That's why I called you the other day. Noreen, I really need you to get back on stage and take the role of Meg in 'Brigadoon.' The girl who had that part just left town without a word. I don't know why, but I had a strange feeling something like that was going to happen. That's why I called you in the first place. I couldn't make the call from here because I didn't want anyone else to know how worried I was. Will you do it? You know that role by heart and no one can dance as well as you. We're in a mess, Noreen. We open tonight."

"Tonight?"

"Yeah, tonight."

"Then I'd better get on stage and start rehearsing."

Marcy threw her arms around the tall, slender woman and gave her a hug.

"You are by far, the best sister I could ever have!"

Aeden

Ajay started to scream the minute it occurred to her that she was touching a dead animal. A large, carnivorous one that had been standing inches from her head.

"A dead thing! A dead thing! I've been holding a dead thing! I can't stand this!"

Then, she realized that Ryn was having a conversation with Hank Clayton and that her great-grandfather was just a few yards away.

"He's alive! Alive! We've got to tell him who we are. Oh my God, he's alive."

"Don't say a word, Ajay," I said as she stepped away from the tiger's body. "Your great-grandfather can never know what happened. It will destroy everything for him. People will never take him seriously again. Understand? He has to think that this was just a hallucination or a dream from getting hit in the head or from falling."

"She's right," Ryn said. "When he plunges forward into time he'll just think that he was knocked out by his kidnapper. That's the way it has to be."

"I just wish I could give him a hug and tell him who I am."

My brother was quick and to the point.

"Yeah, well don't. Under any circumstances."

Hank Clayton started to move towards us and I could see he was still holding the gun at his side. As he got closer to the ledge his voice became clear.

"There should be a road over there and a dirt lot. This ledge is the only thing that looks familiar. And what on earth did I kill? I must be out of my mind."

"You were knocked in the head, somehow," Ryn replied. "It's all in your imagination. It will pass."

Hank started to get closer but something held him back. I could feel it, too. Slight at first, like a wind pressing against my stomach, but then it got stronger. And tighter. I knew without hesitation just what it was.

"Time is moving again," I yelled. "But it's separating us from Hank Clayton."

I took a deep breath because I knew what I had to do next.

Chapter Seventy:
Ryn

~

CRACK! The sound snapped through my body and it took me a moment to figure out what was going on. Time had screamed itself apart and we were standing in the two broken halves that would soon meld again. Ajay, Aeden and I on one side of the rift, and Hank Clayton on the other. Not a visible break but a compression of air and space.

"It's working," I heard myself say as Hank slowly started to disappear from view. Ajay began to shuffle around and I panicked.

"Don't make a move! Don't make a freaking move, Ajay!"

I could see that she had no intention of leaving the spot where she was standing. It was just her nervousness that caused her to move about. But I should have been watching my sister. You'd think by now I would have figured out how unpredictable Aeden had become. In the split second that I yelled at Ajay, Aeden took off with all of her strength to get to the other side of the rift near Hank Clayton.

I thought my lungs would explode.

"WHAT THE HELL ARE YOU DOING?"

"I've got to get back to 1952, Ryn. It's my only chance to make it in theater! Opening night is tonight! And I'm going back."

"AEDEN, DON'T! DON'T----"

But before I could finish my sentence, Ajay blew past me like Lolo Jones chasing after a gold medal. Only Lolo Jones wasn't screaming obscenities.

"The hell you are, Aeden! You're not going to ruin my life. I'm not getting stuck in some primitive time where they don't even have cell phones! I hate 1952 and I'm not staying there another minute!"

Then, Ajay jumped on Aeden's back and wrestled her to the ground. The last time I saw something like this was in seventh grade when two girls got into a fight in the stairwell. I can still remember everyone yelling, "Girl Fight! Girl Fight!" But this time there wasn't a teacher to break it up. Just me, and I had to move fast. They were both edging closer to the rift. One more move and we'd all be stuck in time.

"Back off, Ajay! I've got it!"

I shoved Ajay off of Aeden with enough force to leave me winded. Then, I grabbed my sister by the back of her hair and yanked her towards me. Her elbow jabbed my ribs and I started to cough. Long enough for her to kick me in one of my shins.

"You're going back with us!" I managed to choke out.

"The hell I am!"

Hank Clayton had nearly disappeared from view and the air was getting thick and heavy. Time was trying to move us back to where we belonged. I just had to restrain my sister for a few more seconds. In retrospect, I would have rather been fighting that damn tiger.

Somehow I was able to grab both of her wrists and hold her steady.

"Get closer to us, Ajay!" I shouted.

And then, I felt something tumble on top of me. It was Ajay. She had passed out. And I was too lightheaded to budge. The weight of both of us pressing against Aeden made it impossible for my sister to break away. But not impossible for her to kick and sputter.

I just kept my fingers tight around those wrists and waited for the inevitable thrust back to the 21st century. The pressure on my eyelids was so strong that I winced and held my breath. Aeden finally stopped fighting and I started to relax. Then I remembered something.

Hank Clayton was alive. We had inadvertently altered history. And how the hell we did it, I don't know.

The pressure around me seemed to subside and I felt myself letting go of Aeden's wrists.

Ajay was no longer on top of me but I was petrified to open my eyes.

287

Chapter Seventy-one:
Hank Clayton

Hank Clayton could see the threesome standing under the ledge. At their feet was the saber-tooth tiger he had killed with one bullet. A bullet from the gun that was meant to kill him. As he started to approach the ledge, the air became dense and tight. It was as if something was blocking his every move.

His hands started to tremble as he tried to keep breathing, but the intensity of the air made it impossible. In front of him, the two girls seemed to be struggling. But their movements became wavy and disjointed. Hank struggled to process what was happening.

Then, without warning, he felt as if a coil had grabbed him from the waist, pressing so tight that he was forced to take shallow breaths. And that's the moment he dropped the gun and fell to the ground.

When he opened his eyes again, he heard the familiar noise of birds chirping. The ledge was still there, only it seemed smaller, as if time had eroded it. And no one was standing on or near it.

Hank stood up slowly. His head was pounding and his mouth felt so dry that he could hardly close it. But the dirt lot was only a few feet away and off to one side was the Playhouse truck.

As Hank pulled the door forward, he glanced at the key, still in the ignition. Then he stepped inside and started the engine.

Chapter Seventy-two:
Aeden

I could see swirling patterns of light against my eyelids. As I wiped my hand across my forehead, I felt the dampness from my tears. Ajay's voice bounced all around me and I knew that we were back.

"You've ruined everything, Ryn," I said as I stood up in the small aisle of "The Sun Catcher" store. Ryn was a few feet from me as I bent down to get my purse. It was still in the same spot where I had left it. "I was supposed to get my big break in that performance. Now what are they going to do? It was opening night!"

"Don't get me started, Aeden. First of all, I told you not to get involved with that play. You knew as well as I did that we couldn't guarantee how long we'd be there. And right now, we have worse problems. We don't know what the heck we've done. We came here because they found Ajay's great-grandfather encased in mud. Shot in the head. Only, thanks to us, that never happened. So now what?"

Before I could answer my brother, the clerk, who was in the back of the store, started to walk towards us.

"Ajay! Nice to see you! Looks like you and your friends had a tussle or something. Do you need to use the restrooms?"

"Actually," Ryn blurted out, "we were doing some yard work when my sister realized she needed to buy a gift. And she was so impatient that we all came over here."

"These are my friends," Ajay said, picking up the lead from Ryn. "They're visiting for a few days."

The clerk smiled and continued talking.

"Imagine, arriving in this town just at the time of that gruesome discovery."

"Gruesome?" I could feel my throat creaking.

"Yes, a body encased in mud. Found near old Peccary Pit. Didn't you hear about it, Ajay?"

Ajay shook her head and started to sniffle but the woman continued speaking.

"Can you believe it? They actually were able to identify the poor man."

"Oh my God!"

By now Ajay's sniffling became more audible.

"Oh honey," the woman continued, "It was awful but it turns out that the man was a derelict with quite a long police record. They were able to use dental records that were on file with the police from old prison records. What was that name? Darrell, Darnell...oh well. I'm sure it will be in the papers. Anyway, you folks arrived just in time for the celebration. It's not everyday someone in your family has a bridge named after them. Your grandparents would be so proud if they were still with us today. Imagine, driving over the Hank Clayton Bridge! Why, if it weren't for your great-grandfather, the state never would have connected those highways, allowing for the small cities to merge. Who knows? Even the famous Mark Twain Playhouse might not have survived."

"The Mark Twain Playhouse? The Mark Twain Playhouse?" I stammered.

"Yes, why that's where the Meadows Sisters got their start."

"The Meadows Sisters?" I was still stammering.

"Noreen and Marcy Meadows. But that was way before your time, sweetie. Their big break came in the summer of 1952. My mother saw that musical. Let me think a moment...Oh yes. It was 'Brigadoon.' And after that, those girls went on to Broadway and even some early sitcoms in the 1960s."

I turned and looked directly at Ryn.

"What, Aeden? What do you expect me to say?"

The clerk continued speaking.

"Anyway, all of that was such a long time ago. That summer of 1952 was nothing but one scandal after another. It's a wonder these small communities managed to accomplish anything at all. Anyway, if you need any help, just come get me. I'll be working in the back of the store."

As she headed to her desk, Ajay gave me a quick pat on the shoulder.

"Just think, Aeden, that could have been you! You could have been famous!"

I bit my lower lip and stood still as Ajay continued babbling.

"But what really matters is that we did it! We saved my great-grandfather! He never died. Well, he died eventually, but after living. Oh my God, we changed history!"

Then, she glanced down at her clothes and held up her hands. Her fingernails were chipped and specks of dirt were underneath.

"Look! I'm a wreck! I can't possibly be seen in public! I don't know where to go first – the salon or home."

My brother started to laugh.

"I could tell you where to-----"

But he never got to finish his sentence because I gave him a quick kick in the ankle.

"Get over it, Aeden. I mean it. And Ajay, this is dangerous stuff. You can't breathe a word of it to anyone, ever. Who knows what we've done. Every little change has ramifications that explode exponentially. And if you don't know what that means, get into a math class! I'm happy your great-grandfather lived. But when we walk out the door of this store, everything will be different—the street, the town and even the events leading up to the moment we slipped back to the Ice Age."

For the first time Ajay looked as if she was more interested in something other than herself.

"What do you mean?"

"Hank Clayton was never encased in mud. Some other guy was. So your folks and my mother are not at a police station because none of this happened. When we get back to your house, we just go along with whatever's going on."

"But Ryn," I asked. "Won't our mother know we came here because of that mud discovery?"

"History changed. It changed the moment the time loop began and we met up with Hank Clayton. So Mom's memory and everyone's collective memories will have changed. That's why this is so dangerous."

"You don't have to worry about me shooting off my mouth, Ryn," Ajay said as she tried to wipe some of the dirt off of her fingers. "I don't want people thinking I'm some sort of a nut case. And I meant it, Aeden. You could have been famous."

If we weren't standing in the middle of fancy glass figurines I would have given her a shove! Then, I remembered something – the glass swan and that other figurine.

"Ryn, what happened to the glass animals and the flashlight we were holding?"

"They must have dropped to the ground in that cave, in 1952. Along with the plastic cap gun. Someone probably found those things a long time ago."

"And there's one more thing," I added. "You told Ajay you had an idea of who kidnapped Hank Clayton. Something about the members of the highway commission."

"Sure. Remember when we first got into town and had to take that crossroad from the airport? It was called the 'Brickson-Stockton Road.' And the little tunnel leading into it had a bronze sign on it that said 'FGM' Tunnel. At first I thought it was named after one person. You know, like JFK or MLK. But when Ajay found the articles with the names, I figured out what was going on. The men on that highway commission in 1952 were Raymond Finley, Arthur Gaines, Lloyd Meldridge, and Eugene Brickson. FGM – Finley, Gaines, Meldridge. Add Brickson and what's left? Ed or Tom Stockton. One of them had to be the candidate who would take Hank Clayton's place. I just didn't have time to narrow it down."

Ajay's eyes widened as my brother went on.

"Guess we can forget about Stockton. Or those highways. It's all different. Starting with the Hank Clayton Bridge."

"Oh my God!" Ajay gasped, staring at Ryn.

"What? What's the matter?"

"That nail salon had better be across the street and I'd better have an appointment!"

Chapter Seventy-three: Ryn

Across the aisle, my mother was glued to whatever movie she had downloaded on her iPad. Aeden was still fuming about the whole theater thing and I had just learned that Ajay was going to visit us for an entire two weeks this summer. Talk about a miserable flight home. Still, I figured I needed to set things right with my sister.

"Aeden, you really can't think it's my fault that it wasn't you on that stage."

"I suppose. But I'll never know for sure."

"Well I know. Because it wasn't your time. The Meadows Sisters were meant to get famous. And maybe you will, too. Only in this century, not theirs. Think of the bright side. You still have to perform in that calla lily play."

"Oh my God, I almost forgot! 'Stage Door' opens in three weeks! Three weeks!"

"I think I have practice then."

"Oh no. You owe me. You and Linna are going to sit through every performance."

"Don't punish my girlfriend. She had nothing to do with this!"

"Punish? She should be thrilled to see me now, because in ten years she won't be able to afford the tickets!"

"Dream on, Aeden."

I shut my eyes and started to doze off when I felt a poke in my side.

"I don't think we should be doing this time travel stuff anymore. It was one thing to be a spectator, but now that we know we can change things, it's too scary."

"What do you say we lock the formulas up for now and talk about it when we're really old – like after college?"

"Yeah, after college. Unless..."

"Yeah...unless."

And then I closed my eyes again and let my body drift off to the steady hum of the plane's engine. After college...geez. I'll be ancient by then.

* * *

University of Missouri, Department of Geological Sciences Office of Professor Howard Langston, Paleontological, Sedimentological and Stratigraphy Studies, Present Day

*I*t's a Doctor Wesley Jamison from Texas A & M on the phone for you, Professor Langston."

"Thanks, Sheila. Put him through."

Howard Langston listened intently to what Dr. Jamison had to say. Then, when he put down the receiver, he motioned for his assistant.

"Cal, remember when we sent that sample of the partial saber-tooth skull to Elemental Analysis at Texas A & M a few months ago?"

"Sure, I recommended that lab in the first place. Why? Did something go wrong?"

"No. Not exactly. But they found the same results we did. Only they sent their own team of geologists to the dig site near Springfield. And you'll never guess what they uncovered."

Cal shrugged his shoulders and waited for his boss to continue.

"They found the usual stuff – bone fragments and the like. And they also took back some larger rock samples for analysis. But when they put one of them through the mass spectrometer, they realized that underneath the layers of rock was a gun. The size and shape of a 38 caliber gun. And if I'm not mistaken, that size bullet would match the hole we found in the partial skull."

"But that's impossible. The rock samples date back to the Ice Age."

"Hold your breath, Cal. I'm usually a skeptic when it comes to these things, but now I'm not so sure. The evidence is pretty clear – someone found a way back in time. I just hope they know what they're doing."

THE END

ENDNOTES

Missouri Highway Department

The state of Missouri did indeed have a department of transportation and a highway commission. The Missouri Highways and Transportation Commission is a six-member bipartisan board, not a five-member board as derived in this fictional novel.

In 1952, the state began a ten-year program entitled "The Missouri 10-Year Highway Modernization and Expansion Program," for the purpose of upgrading and incorporating roads so that rural areas would have access to state maintained roads. The program received the nickname, "The Takeover Program."

For more information, please visit Missouri Department of Transportation
http://www.modot.org

The Ice Age

Current scientific belief holds that the "Ice Age" began 2.6 million years ago during the Pleistocene Epoch of the Cenozoic Era (65.5 million years ago).

A number of large mammals, including mastodons, saber-tooth tigers, peccaries, short-faced bears, and the giant sloth all lived in what is now the state of Missouri during that time.

WORKS CITED

en.wikipedia.org/wiki/Ice_age

en.wikipedia.org/wiki/Lawdy_Miss_Clawdy

**www.chemguide.co.uk/analysis/massp
ec/howitworks.html**

www.fiftiesweb.com

www.historyoftheuniverse.com

www.modot.org

www.riverbluffcave.com

www.slfp.com/Mastodon.htm

**www.ucmp.berkeley.edu/quaternary/
pleistocene.php**

STUDY GUIDE:

Light Riders and the Missouri Mud Murder

This young adult adventure blends historical and science fiction. The study guide component provides teachers with differentiated questions and activities designed to develop thinking skills and promote a better understanding of these particular eras in time. The study guide is reproducible for classroom use.

Introduction and Chapters One – Five

1. Why does Professor Langston believe there is a problem with the mass spectrometer?
2. Do you know what a mass spectrometer does? Explain.
3. Why don't Ryn and Aeden want to spend time with Ajay? Have you ever felt that way about anyone?
4. How does Ryn convince his sister that they will be able to travel back in time to the correct year? Do you agree?
5. Yes or No. Ajay is self-centered. Explain and give an example.

6. List three verbs that describe Aeden's reaction when she finds out where time really took them.
7. How does Ajay explain what happened?

Chapters Six – Ten

1. What is the Pleistocene epoch? Can you draw a geographical timeline to show this epoch? (Hint – Think Cenozoic Era)
2. Find three popular songs from 1951 – 1952. Have you ever heard any of them?
3. Why doesn't Ajay believe that they are still in the past? How does she eventually find out?
4. Why do Ryn and Aeden pretend to be the new theater crew members? What would you do if you were in their position?
5. Do you think Aeden is going to wind up acting in the summer theater?
6. Why is it inadvisable to alter history (even if you could)?

Chapters Eleven – Fifteen

1. Aeden wakes up with a strong sense of dread. Has something like this ever happened to you? Explain.

2. If you knew that someone was hiding a gun, what would you do?
3. Name at least three animals that lived during the Ice Age.
4. Should Ryn be worried that the time-space continuum is wobbling?
5. Yes or No. Ajay was right to sneak out in order to warn her great-grandfather. Justify your answer.
6. What is the irony regarding the proposed placement of the new highway?
7. Why doesn't Aeden trust Ajay?

Chapters Sixteen – Twenty

1. List three things Ryn found out from Owen at the lumberyard.
2. Aeden says that "time is like an oyster." Pick another simile and re-write Aeden's explanation that appears at the end of chapter seventeen.
3. If you were behind the wheel instead of Ryn, what would you have done?
4. Where did the dead animal really come from?
5. Who do you think might have switched the guns?

Chapters Twenty-one – Twenty-five

1. Should Ryn and Aeden have told the truth to Ajay about their time travel?
2. Why is Dr. Wesley Jamison so concerned about the results from three of the labs at Texas A & M? * Do you know what Texas A & M is?
3. If you were Hank Clayton, would you have told someone about the threats you were getting? Why or why not?
4. Is Ryn really jealous of his sister?
5. The summer theater is producing the play *Brigadoon.* What is so ironic about that play? (If you find the synopsis, you'll figure it out!)
6. Do you think the kidnapping and theft are related?
7. Write a sentence that describes Darnell Legrun's character traits.
8. Should Aeden have accepted the role in the play? Why or why not?

Chapters Twenty-six – Thirty

1. How does Darnell Legrun justify his actions?
2. What really happened in the theater?
3. Should Marcy be trusted? Explain.

4. If you were Ryn, would you have told Aeden and Ajay the truth about the time loop?

5. Do you think it's OK for people to hide the truth from others? Explain and give examples.

Chapters Thirty-one – Thirty-five

1. Aeden says that her brother "grits his teeth and glares when he doesn't get his way." Describe someone you know and what they do when they don't get their way. Or, describe what you do!

2. Have you ever eavesdropped on anyone? Do you think it was the right thing for Ryn to do?

3. Why did Ajay lie and tell Nick that she, Ryn and Aeden were good splelunkers?

4. "Splelunkers" was the word used years ago to describe seasoned cave explorers. What word is used today?

5. Why does Aeden agree to go to the caves?

6. Why was there water in the cave?

7. Ajay finishes Ryn's sentence at the end of chapter thirty-five with the words "swallowed Hank Clayton back to the Ice Age." Replace the work "swallow" with another verb.

Chapters Thirty-six- Forty

1. Who wrote *The Adventures of Tom Sawyer?* (Hint – the author's name appears in this novel).
2. Yes or no. Marcy Meadows is overreacting. Explain.
3. If you were in Ryn's position, what would you have taken into the cave and why? (Remember, this is 1952).
4. Darnell Legrun believed he had four options and none of them good. Do you think there were other alternatives for him?
5. Write a complete sentence describing how you picture Councilman Barkley. What would be his physical traits and his personality traits?

Chapters Forty-one – Forty-five

1. Why was Ajay so terrified of Ryn's decision at the end of chapter forty-one? Is she being self-centered or logical?
2. Re-write the first sentence in chapter forty-two by replacing the words "thundered" and "running." How do words affect the mood of a story?

3. Find at least two examples of figurative language (i.e. metaphor, simile, allusion, onomatopoeia, alliteration, etc.) in chapter forty-three.
4. What finally happens to Darnell Legrun?
5. Would you have taken the same chance that Ryn did, in order to save his sister?

Chapters Forty-six- Fifty

1. Who's hiding something? Marcy or Clarisse? Explain.
2. Do you believe Ajay will ever find her great-grandfather? Why or why not?
3. Ryn says that the red and white checkered sleeve will give him nightmares. Can you think of any images in books or movies that give you nightmares?
4. Why did the volunteers believe Ryn when he explained that the bear was just a reflection?
5. Should Ajay be worried about Aeden's preoccupation with the play?

Chapters Fifty-one – Fifty-five

1. How do you think Ryn is going to figure out who killed Hank Clayton?

2. Yes or no. Ryn gave Ajay a clever clue about the meeting time.
3. Do you think Ryn should have been so direct with Phil? Have you ever accused someone of something only to learn that they didn't do it?
4. Yes or no. Clarisse did the right thing by hiding the gun for her brother. Explain.
5. Who was Albert Einstein and who is Stephen Hawking?

Chapters Fifty-six – Sixty

1. Yes or no. Ryn did the right thing by taking the truck. Explain your reasoning.
2. What are pill bugs? Where are they found?
3. What really happened to Hank Clayton?
4. Does Hank Clayton realize that he has gone back in time?
5. Can you justify Clarisse's actions regarding the theft? Does the end justify the means?
6. Ryn, Aeden and Ajay see the checkered cloth for the second time. How is their reaction different from the first?

Chapters Sixty-one- Sixty-five

1. What was the real intent of Bob Barkley's plan? Who was or were the real mastermind(s)?
2. In chapter sixty-four, Hank Clayton sees the outline of a creature. What was he really seeing?
3. Who is more dramatic – Aeden or Ajay? Give at least two examples to support your choice.

Chapters Sixty-six – Seventy

1. Why does Hank believe that he had been shot?
2. How does the phase "just in the nick of time," apply to chapter sixty-seven ?
3. What was Marcy Meadows really worried about?
4. Why doesn't Ryn want Ajay to tell Hank the truth about who she is?
5. What do you suppose might have happened if Aeden had managed to stay in 1952?

Chapters Seventy-one – Seventy-three and Conclusion

1. Chapter seventy-one ends with an inference. What do you suppose happened to Hank?
2. Describe Aeden's reaction when she learns about the famous Meadows sisters.
3. Who were the real Meadows sisters? (Hint – Ajay's 1952 name).
4. How did Ryn, Aeden and Ajay manage to alter history? What changed? Why do you suppose it changed?
5. Name at least two bridges or roads in your state that were named after someone famous.
6. Do you think Ryn and Aeden should use time travel again? Justify your answer. **Share your answer at: lightriders@timetravelmysteries.com**
7. What has Professor Howard Langston figured out?

THEMATIC CLASSROOM PROJECTS

1. Compare and contrast living in 1952 with living today. (Foods, clothing, entertainment, music, education, travel, family life, etc.) * Be sure to include the attitude towards smoking.
2. Create a geological timeline for the Pleistocene Epoch.
3. Draw your version of the Mark Twain Playhouse.
4. Research universities that offer studies in paleontology, sedimentology and stratigraphy. Seek opportunities to visit their labs.
5. Select at least one extinct creature from the Ice Age and describe how it lived.
6. "Stage Door" was a real play and a real movie. What was it about? What famous red-haired comedian appeared in it?
7. The Mark Twain Playhouse produced two plays and one musical during the 1952 season in this novel. Read at least one of those plays before you graduate from high school!

ACKNOWLEDGEMENTS

Thank you, Gale Leach, from Two Cats Press, for bringing Time Travel Mysteries into your fold.

I am indeed grateful to my editors and proof-readers for their diligence, commitment and expertise. Susan Morrow and Steve Somers in New York and Susan Schwartz in Brisbane, Australia, for their attention to logistics, flow and continuity. Not to mention their amazing mastery of the lexicon. And to Ellen Lynes in Pennsylvania, Suzanne Scher in Florida, and Lisa Tonks in Arizona for their focus on detail, nuance, and style. This book would not have been possible without your support.

And to my husband and favorite critic, James E. Clapp, whose encouragement never waivers.

ABOUT THE AUTHOR

Arizona author and New York native Ann I. Goldfarb has written six young adult mystery-suspense novels. Her first novel, *The Face Out of Time*, received an award in 2011 from the Arizona Authors Association and her third novel, *The Last Tag*, was a finalist in the New Mexico-Arizona Book Awards.

The author spent most of her career in education, first as a classroom teacher and later as a school principal and staff developer. Her non-fiction works have appeared in a number of trade magazines for Jones Publishing and Madavor Media, which was later incorporated into Jones Publishing.

Writing to entice and engage readers has always been a passion for her.

Ann resides with her family near the foothills of the White Tank Mountains in Arizona.